The Tales of Nesterhoffen

Baron Otto

Contents

About the Author

Baron Otto is one of several pen names used by the author. A screenwriter, short story writer as well as a song writer and inventor. A traveler who moves with the changing of seasons and the changing of moods. Born in America to German immigrant parents.

The Tales of Nesterhoffen shows the romantic heart and philosophical soul of the author. The clever use of political satire at the start resembles Jonathan Swift's world of Lilliput in Gulliver's Travels, where two kings were ready to go to war over which end of an egg to break.

VILLAGE RHYME

Four ancient hags tried to
steal a goose, but a little
village girl wouldn't turn
it loose. All the village
men put the hags to flight.
Four hungry hags will eat
no goose tonight

Prologue

On a crisp, early June evening near midnight in the year 1242 A.D., two ramshackled gypsy carts stood parked by a campfire on the outskirts of a tiny Bavarian village.

Crouched about this campfire were four extremely old and horribly misshapen hags, each more bent, twisted and gnarled than the other. Yet none so ugly as the one who led the rest in some kind of unholy ritual.

Chanting and swaying from side to side, this loathsome demon of barely human shape occasionally pulled something from an unsightly pouch at her waist and cast it upon the fire. The flames rose and gave off all manner of eerie colors while dancing high like tortured phantom spirits.

"No milk of human kindness abides here," her snarling voice rasped out. So saying, she poured a cup of vile milky substance upon the fire. The flames leaped up in a frightening greenish hue in answer while the other three hags chanted and poured more corruption upon the fire.

> "For want of seed, there
> is no grain; for want of
> grain, there is no goose.
> For want of a goose,
> there is no supper."

Thus said, another portion of black magic from the pouch was cast upon the fire, and the fire boiled with a cold, hungry flame.

Baron Otto

"If there is this night no supper, for want of charity to give one goose, then I say, that if there is no goose, there can be no egg."

Another handful from the pouch, another chorus from the three consorts and yet another fiery dance of evil light followed her words.

"To those peasants who give me no supper this night, I give them no kindness in return."

And as she dusted the fire into an evil blaze, she proclaimed the following curse:

"Low little village of little men with no charity, behold the kingdom I give you."

Her hands did fly as the fire burnt high.

"I shall build for you a joyous castle upon your very doorstep, and you shall not want for anything."

Again, from pouch to pyre, as flames grew high and higher.

"And when my seeds are sown,
when all your grain is ripe and grown,
when the geese are fatted and ready for the pot,
then I shall come and steal the lot."

A chorus of evil cackling pleasure rippled about the campfire.

"For I shall steal the egg
by which you measure all
your prosperity and joy."

Rising to her full, if crippled height and casting up her arms and hideous face, she proclaimed,

"Behold Nesterhoffen, I bring you your Heaven and your Hell. For want of one supper's charity, I give you a lifetime of affliction."

Pausing, once again crouching near the vile sickness of her eerie blaze, she placed this final part of her curse on the poor, unsuspecting villagers.

"By night, by fire,
by devil's own desire,
I chain you to this curse.
Let no man break these chains by which I bind you,
lest he be of Nesterhoffen
and would give his life for charity's sake."

—-And so, the Tales of Nesterhoffen began.

Baron Otto

PRONUNCIATION OF NAMES

ARNO:	ARE – NO
ELFRIEDE:	L – FREE – dah
EMMA:	M – AH
EWALD:	A – walt
GOTTHARDT:	Goot – heart
HORST:	HORSED
INGA:	Ing – AH
ISHMAN:	ISH-MEN
JOHAN:	Yo – Hun
JON:	Yon
KAAN:	CAN
LIZELLE:	Leaze – ul
LUDWIG:	Lewed – wick
NESTERHOFFEN:	NESS – tur – how- fin
OSKAR:	OH – SCAR
REEMISS:	RHEE – miss
SALZBURG:	SAULS – berg
WASSERBURG:	WAH – sir -berg

PART 1:
THE PRINCE AND THE PRINCESS

Chapter I: The Meek and the Mighty

Long, long ago, nestled in the vast Bavarian forests, amid the towering mountains near Austria, there was a small peaceful village named Nesterhoffen. In this tiny village, tucked far away from the mainstream of human events, a few peasant farmers worked diligently to provide themselves with a meager living.

Sixty industrious souls labored very hard to produce a fairly good cheese, a better-than-average sausage, and harvest exceptionally sought-after hops. On these three items, the farmers of Nesterhoffen depended on for the success and prosperity of their village. But, most of all, they relied on the warm, early spring season to ensure a large and healthy harvest of their hops fields. This crop was their main source of income and was highly prized by the brewers of Austria and Bavaria.

Should a long, cold winter linger late into the spring with great drifts of snow covering the land, stunting the growth of the hops fields, the villagers of Nesterhoffen were bound to suffer a lean and hungry year. Fortunately, these lean years were few, and the small village was a happy and prosperous place.

Yet, there was something about the village of Nesterhoffen that was of even greater importance than the hops. Of this, the villagers themselves were totally unaware.

It concerned the narrow, winding, mountain pass that led from Salzburg in Austria to Wasserburg in Bavaria and ran right through the middle of Nesterhoffen. For whoever controlled the mountain pass at Nesterhoffen controlled the invasion route into Austria or Bavaria.

To the peasants of Nesterhoffen, this poorly kept road was only a way to be traveled each fall to bring their harvest to market. But, for King Ewald Herman Gotthardt of Salzburg and King Karl Wilhelm Von Nickolaus of Wasserburg, the pass through Nesterhoffen was a source of great concern and many sleepless nights.

Though the two small kingdoms had been at peace with each other for many years, both were extremely wary of each other. For kings of that time had a fondness for mistrusting each other and generally walked about casting nervous glances behind them.

Neither king was willing to go to war with the other for control of the pass at Nesterhoffen, for whoever should lose such a war would almost certainly lose his kingdom as well. And neither of these noble monarchs was brave enough to risk so much.

So King Karl of Bavaria would worry and fret, while King Ewald of Austria would fret and worry, while the unsuspecting villagers of Nesterhoffen slept peacefully in their goose-down beds.

However, on any given summer's night, both kings were apt to sleep fitfully, with nightmares of invading armies marching through the pass of Nesterhoffen. Each king would rise early the next morning, grab the first officer he might find loitering outside his bedroom chamber and demand that the officer ride to Nesterhoffen to check on the hops fields.

Of course, this was just a ploy. It was the king's way of saying, "Go to Nesterhoffen and find out if we're being invaded!" Kings had a way of not saying what they meant and not meaning what they said.

Then, each of them winked at the officer to be sure he understood. King Ewald always winked with his left eye, while King Karl always winked with his right eye.

From the time the snows melted off the pass at Nesterhoffen in the spring until the snows of the following fall closed the road again for winter, many would be the days that the villagers of Nesterhoffen were visited by soldiers from both these kingdoms, checking on the condition of the hops fields.

If the villagers of Nesterhoffen were curious at this single-minded tendency of kings, it worried them not. The more the soldiers came to inspect their hops fields, the higher would be the prices they could charge for their harvest in the fall, and the more willing the brewers would be to pay outrageous prices for the hops. The brewers couldn't help knowing how concerned their kings were with the hops at Nesterhoffen. Why else would both kings keep their ends of the road to Nesterhoffen closed to all other merchants and travelers? Surely, then, the hops at Nesterhoffen must be the finest hops in the whole world!

King Karl and King Ewald each kept their end of the road closed for fear of spies and hidden armies masquerading as merchants or travelers.

Plagued as the kings were by ceaseless nightmares about the pass at Nesterhoffen, neither king cared one whit about the hops that grew there.

But if this dilemma was a curse for kings, it was also a curse for the happy, hard-working villagers of Nesterhoffen. For, in the fall, after their hops had been harvested and sold, half in Wasserburg and half in Salzburg, an emissary from both kingdoms arrived at

Nesterhoffen. Then, the industrious peasants had to pay taxes – not to one king but to two!

In this way, both kings laid claim to Nesterhoffen, yet avoided going to war over it. As bad as the nightmares of these royal kings might be, they were mere unpleasant dreams to the poor, hard-working villagers. The nightmares of the peasants were real, not imagined. They knew, without a doubt, that come each fall, not one tax collector, but two, would arrive in their tiny village.

Baron Otto

<u>And such are the dilemmas of the mighty and the meek.</u>

<u>A solution so small as an ounce of trust they seek.</u>

Chapter II: Mother Nature Has a Plan

Mother Nature, given time, has a way of adjusting all things in life. In the spring of that long, long ago, Mother Nature provided such a glorious and wonderful spring that no one in the village could remember it's like. The warm golden days of sunshine seemed endless, and the sparkling clear night skies were occasionally interrupted by soft, gentle rains of just the right duration: all things flourished in and around Nesterhoffen. The abundance was such that all those who lived there were astonished and amazed.

The village women sniffed the crisp, clean mountain air, and their hearts fluttered to the perfumed fragrances of wild mountain violets and edelweiss. Meanwhile, the men sighed with pleasure over the pungent scents of pine and hop blossoms, though mostly they sighed over the hop blossoms.

The abundance of that spring was not only of the fields and flowers. Willie Koch, the cheese maker, was delighted by the fat, healthy new calves in his small dairy herd, while the sows of Adolf Gruber, the sausage maker, produced litters so prodigious that poor Adolf could only scratch his bald head in blissful wonderment. And Johan Kruger's pretty young daughters, Gretchen, Greta, and Gertrude, raced about the village herding their immense flocks of goslings.

But most of all, it was a spring that made love bloom. Many were the courtships of May and June. Even the homeliest farm boy or most ungainly village girl seemed to blossom with a newfound beauty.

When Otto Bauer, the innkeeper, village elder, and long-time widower, married the village spinster, Lizelle Betcher, everyone knew that this was a spring glorious beyond compare. But Mother Nature had only just begun.

Indeed, this wondrous spring was only the window dressing for a much greater event.

That spring, in the castle of King Karl of Bavaria, King Karl's son, Prince Ludwig Johann Von Nickolaus, had reached his eighteenth year of age. He had also become a growing nuisance and desperate concern to his father.

The boy's been spoiled so badly by his poor departed mother, thought the pudgy little king, that he's as useless as a one-legged horse.

Prince Ludwig wandered about all day, staring into space, and rarely had enough wits about him to answer to his own name. King Karl wondered wearily, what sort of dullard son have I been given?

When the boy should have been training with sword and lance, he was off moping in some forest in the hills. And while King Karl's best advisors sat patiently waiting to teach Prince Ludwig the business of ruling the kingdom, he was off on the lake, alone in a small boat, daydreaming and rowing in circles. The boy is a hopeless waste! King Karl of Bavaria thought.

Yet, if King Karl had a difficult time trying to understand his son, then King Ewald of Salzburg found it twice as difficult to understand his beautiful young daughter.

Princess Inga of Salzburg wandered about the flower beds of her father's castle all day picking flowers, then arranging useless bouquets, only to pluck all the petals off the flowers while humming sad old songs to herself.

Perhaps if King Ewald's wife had lived, she could have explained Princess Inga to him. As it was, poor King Ewald was totally confused by his sad, sulking daughter.

Could my poor daughter have injured her head in some way, worried the tall, slender king as he stroked his beard in contemplation. Or possibly she's contracted some new sickness or has been bewitched by those accursed dwarfs who live deep in the woods, he wondered.

When the best advice his physicians and counselors could give him was, "She may only be lonely, your Highness," King Ewald flew into a towering rage and chased them all from the castle.

"Lonely, indeed!" thought the king. Princess Inga had more servants, maids, ladies-in-waiting, doting aunts and cousins than any ten princesses. In fact, most of the meager taxes King Ewald collected went to feed the endless gabbling hordes of people about the castle who made sure that Princess Inga, above all else, was never lonely.

"Lonely, indeed!" thought the bewildered king; "I should have chopped all their empty heads off for advice like that!"

But Mother Nature was undaunted by these trivial complaints from mere kings. She knew what was troubling the young prince and princess. And the beautiful and wondrous spring that she had provided was, at the same time, the cause and the cure.

Baron Otto

For Mother Nature, in her own day,

will spread her light and guide your way.

Chapter III: Melancholy Youth

Once again, King Karl of Bavaria arose in a disturbed state. Fearing his kingdom was about to be attacked, he jumped from his bed and went in search of the first officer of his castle whom he might find idling about. Someone had to check on the hops fields of Nesterhoffen.

Now, all the officers in the castle of King Karl enjoyed this duty immensely: long ago, they had decided to take turns idling about near the king's chamber each morning. Not only was the ride a pleasant change from their usual duties, but they all enjoyed visiting with the happy, friendly people who lived in the tiny village of Nesterhoffen, … especially the farmers' pretty, young daughters.

On this particular day, the good fortune fell to a young officer named Arno who also happened to be Prince Ludwig's best friend. As Arno was fetching his horse for the ride to Nesterhoffen, he chanced to think how unhappy his friend, young Prince Ludwig, had been of late.

Returning to the presence of King Karl, he ventured, "Your Highness, forgive me, but perhaps if Prince Ludwig were to ride with me to Nesterhoffen, it might cheer him up."

Young Arno would greatly enjoy having his friend ride beside him. "The weather's beautiful," he added quickly, trying to persuade the king to allow the prince this chance to get out of the castle for a while.

Though Arno was the youngest of the officers at King Karl's castle, with his short, curly hair and puppy brown eyes, he was a favorite among all the officers and men. Arno was always cheerful, a fountain of laughter and good humor.

King Karl knew these things well about young Arno, as he knew that Arno was his son's best friend. And, if nothing else these days, that alone gave King Karl great solace. King Karl, too, liked his impetuous young officer.

Now, as the king looked at the radiant excitement on young Arno's face, he could not help being infected by the boy's bright expectations. A smile spread slowly across his own face. "That's a most excellent idea, Office Arno! Why don't you find that worthless son of mine and tell him I've ordered him to ride with you? You'd better take an escort along," he added, thinking Arno might need help should his dullard son fall off his horse.

"Oh! He's not worthless, Sire," Arno spoke up quickly. "Not at all. And thank you, Sire… thank you," called Arno over his shoulder, for he was already running off to find his friend, Prince Ludwig.

King Karl could only shake his head and laugh at this impetuous and personable young man and wish that his son were more like him.

***

As fate would have, King Ewald of Salzburg also arose early that morning with visions of armies marching against him through the pass at Nesterhoffen. His officers were no less intelligent than the officers in Bavaria; they also took turns idling about each morning near their king's bed chamber in hopes of being picked to ride to Nesterhoffen.

On that particular day, it was the turn of a tall, slender, and dark-haired officer named, Horst. Horst was nearly twenty-six years old and extremely conscientious and contemplative in nature. He was very slow to speak or give his opinion, but this was only because he thought through each question or idea thoroughly before he would answer. For this reason, he was highly regarded for his advice and opinion, even unto the king.

So, when a worried King Ewald spied Horst idling about near his bed chamber, he was much relieved. "Pssst, Horst!" King Ewald beckoned from the doorway of his bed chamber. "Come here. I have an errand for you."

Although Horst did not smile openly, his spirits certainly did, for he already knew what errand his king must want of him. And Horst, like all the other officers of both kingdoms, also greatly enjoyed the ride to Nesterhoffen.

But Horst was still surprised by the request of his king. For King Ewald had seen enough of his beautiful young daughter's melancholy and was determined to do something about it.

"Is the road to Nesterhoffen a dangerous ride?" asked King Ewald as soon as Horst had entered his chambers.

"No, Your Highness," said Horst after pausing first to think of the state of the narrow little road that led to Nesterhoffen.

"As a matter of fact, it should be a very pleasant ride on such a beautiful day like today," slowly added Horst.

"Hmmm…." mulled the king as he stroked his beard and paced about. "Would there be any danger to my daughter if she were to ride there?" asked King Ewald as he impatiently waited for Horst to answer.

"No, Your Highness," finally answered Horst, after due deliberation. "With a proper escort along, there should be no danger whatsoever…. and," paused Horst,… "she may even find the ride a pleasant diversion." For King Ewald was not the only one in Salzburg to have noticed Princess Inga's melancholy.

"Good," thought King Ewald as he stroked his beard and paced while his mind continued to search for any problems that might arise if he were to send his daughter on a ride to Nesterhoffen. For King Ewald, though constantly bewildered by his daughter, still loved her most dearly and would protect her from all harm, whether real or imagined.

"But are the villagers friendly?" queried the king.

To answer this question, even slow, conscientious, Horst didn't need time to think. For no sooner was the question asked than a vision of Gretchen Kruger, the eldest daughter of the hops farmer whose three daughters raised geese, came into his head… beautiful Gretchen, with her bright blue eyes and long blonde braids.

"Oh, yes, Your Highness. They are most friendly," replied Horst so quickly that even King Ewald was taken by surprise. For Horst was losing the battle to control his emotions with such a beautiful vision floating about in his head. A sheepish smile slowly spread across his face while his ears blushed red.

"You're sure?" asked a confused King Ewald, for never before had he seen this trusted officer so eager with an answer.

"Truly, Your Highness. They are among the happiest and kindest people in your entire kingdom." Horst answered with such honesty and sincerity that even King Ewald was convinced.

"Good…Very good." replied the king. "Here's what I want you to do." King Ewald placed a fatherly arm about Horst's shoulders and paced about the room with him. "I want you to help me get my daughter to stop all this foolish moping about. I want you to pick an escort for her… and I think her cousin, Eleanor…"

"Yes," Horst agreed. "Yes, indeed, her cousin Eleanor… Princess Eleanor is always so gay and witty, and she is Princess Inga's favorite friend."

King Ewald, having solved one minor dilemma, stopped to stroke his beard. "Best make sure the escort is made up of officers of good humor, as well as proficiency at arms." The king left no small matters to chance. "And make sure she rides a gentle horse…"

"And don't forget to check the hops fields… "And don't be late in getting back…

"And be wary of rock slides and robbers… "And don't go near any dwarfs…

"And this, and that, and more!" shouted King Ewald from his balcony as Horst and his small party rode out of hearing.

***

As devoted as Horst was to his king, he was doubly so in his devotion to the beautiful young Princess Inga, as were all the officers in the castle of King Ewald. They thought of her as a favorite younger sister or daughter.

For this reason, Horst had encountered a bit of difficulty in selecting the six officers he needed for the Princess' escort. Each and every officer wanted to make the trip. Finally, Horst had solved the problem by taking those six officers who would have been the next in turns to be idling about the king's bed chamber each morning.

On the road to Nesterhoffen their mood was frivolous and gay as they waved for the last time to the shouting King Ewald.

Now Horst was beset with lovely visions of Gretchen Kruger again. He was looking forward to seeing her with a good deal of blushing anticipation. Meanwhile, he suffered the friendly jesting of his fellow officers who knew of his secret love for the pretty farm girl.

Princess Eleanor, Princess Inga's closest friend and confidant, though she was almost three years older and lived in her father's castle in Vienna most of the year, was as delightful and cheerful as she was pretty. She enjoyed the company of the seven officers with their good manners and charming wit.

As for the young officers, no one could have been enjoying themselves more. To be chosen for the ride to Nesterhoffen on an ordinary day and to ride there by oneself was cause for joy. But to be riding there on such a marvelous spring day with two beautiful princesses for company, well, suffice to say, they were overcome with pleasure.

They all laughed and enjoyed the sunshine and each other's company; all, that is, except Princess Inga. Though she smiled politely at their humor, she didn't laugh; she moped along, her mood dreary and her mind burdened with dismal thoughts.

The melancholy of youth is only a passing thing;

just the pause it takes the eye to aim while,

cupid draws his string.

Chapter IV: Love's Sweet Bloom

Much as Mother Nature had intended, Princess Inga and her small group from Austria arrived in Nesterhoffen at the precise same time as Prince Ludwig and his small group from Bavaria. As Horst led his party from Salzburg into the village from the east, he immediately saw Arno leading his party from Wasserburg into the village from the west. Never before had soldiers from either kingdom seen so many of the other's troops near this vital pass. Both Horst of Austria and Arno of Bavaria were struck by fear, the fear that they had finally encountered that which their kings had dreaded most – an invasion army.

Arno, so young and frivolous on most occasions, was nevertheless quick-minded and well-trained. He acted first, telling his men to stand their horses in a line in front of their Prince. Then he rode forward alone into the center of Nesterhoffen with his hand held high in the signal of peace.

Horst, fearing for the safety of Princesses Inga and Eleanor, hissed orders to the other officers to take up position in a line in front of the two young ladies where they might protect them should the girls need to flee. Then, leaving one of the other young officers in charge and ordering that, under penalty of death, nothing should harm the two princesses, he rode forward slowly, his arm raised in the gesture of peace.

In the middle of the village, the two nervous and perplexed officers met and introduced themselves.

The villagers of Nesterhoffen had never seen so many soldiers before. They knew nothing of wars or bloodshed. Soon, all those villagers about were gazing at this grand spectacle in an awe of curious dumbfoolery; all, that is, but old Otto Bauer's new wife, the once shy and retiring spinster, Lizelle.

Though Lizelle had only been married a few short weeks, she had quickly understood the workings of her husband's inn and knew how profitable it could be with a somewhat larger trade. As Horst and Arno faced one another on their horses directly in front of the inn, Lizelle took matters into her own hands. While Horst and Arno queried each other suspiciously, yet politely, about why the other had so many soldiers in Nesterhoffen, Lizelle quickly drew two large steins of beer from a keg inside the inn and walked out into the roadway between the two officers. She offered one to each, compliments of the inn, apologizing for the absence of her husband, Otto, who was off working in the hops fields.

With Lizelle's intervention, Arno and Horst relaxed a bit, realizing they were both in Nesterhoffen on a friendly mission, though each was still confused by the number of the other's cadre. Though each answered the other's questions politely and truthfully about being in Nesterhoffen to check the condition of the hops fields, neither volunteered that they were escorts for their respective prince or princess. Since the Bavarian soldiers sat on their horses in front of Prince Ludwig and the soldiers of Salzburg had formed a line before the princesses, neither Horst nor Arno could see them. But the plans of Mother Nature were not to be forestalled by the suspicions of a paltry handful of soldiers.

At that moment, the eldest daughter of Johan Kruger, the lovely Gretchen, ran up from the fields and skidded to a stop by the side of Horst, who still sat on his horse in perplexed contemplation. With a breathless, happy laugh and a smile that would melt the heart of a troll, she announced, "Horst, it's so good to see you again. You must have dinner with us. My father and mother would be so pleased. Say yes, please? Horst, you'd make them so happy. And… and we're having a roast goose and dumplings… and… oh… and everything!"

Though her parents, who had met Horst and liked him, would enjoy his company at dinner, they certainly hadn't planned to have goose and dumplings and everything on a Wednesday.

But, if Horst can be forgiven for his secret love for this pretty, blue-eyed farmer's daughter, then surely Gretchen can be forgiven for being so deeply and not so secretly in love with this handsome cavalry officer.

At the sight of Gretchen's breathless beauty, Horst forgot completely about Arno and his soldiers from Bavaria. "I cannot," he said painfully. "I must stay and guard Princess Inga." Suddenly, Horst realized that a soldier from Bavaria was listening. Aghast at his own blunder and on the verge of drawing his sword, he feared the Bavarians would try to take Princess Inga hostage and hold her for ransom.

Gretchen, blithely unaware of the danger and paying no notice of Arno, said, "Bring her to dinner, too," as if having the Royal Princess of Salzburg to dinner was a common occurrence at the Kruger farmhouse.

Suddenly Arno realized that Horst and his soldiers were only an escort, just as his own men. He could no longer contain his humorous spirit, especially with the pretty farm girl making Horst blush a brilliant red. In a burst of friendly laughter, he dismounted and gathered the two large steins of beer from the bewildered Lizelle. Offering one to Horst, who still sat on his horse in the crimson confusion, Arno confessed to him that he and his men were but an escort for their prince. Thus, the situation explained itself.

Horst dismounted to join Arno in laughter and a mutual toast to their kings and countries, and pretty Gretchen, who could not be dissuaded by a few princes and princesses, said, "Shall I tell Mother that you'll stay for dinner, then?"

Arno could stand no more. Laughing so hard he could barely stand, he placed an arm around the shoulders of the blushing, grinning Horst. Soon, the comedy of the scene became known to all as Horst, Gretchen, and Lizelle laughed just as loudly and happily.

"Herr Horst," said Arno after catching his breath. "Perhaps if Frau Bauer would be so kind, our men could put their arms in her back room until we depart. Then your princess might like to wash herself after your long ride and have something to eat at the inn."

"Oh, yes," agreed Lizelle quickly, excited by the idea of having a real princess in her inn. Before Horst or Arno could stop her, Lizelle ran off toward the soldiers from Salzburg to invite the princess to the inn. This sent Arno, Horst and Gretchen into another fit of laughter.

Heinz, the officer in charge of the escort for the princesses, had watched cautiously as the meeting took place in the center of Nesterhoffen. As Horst and the Bavarian soldier had dismounted and joined in laughter, sharing steins of beer together, he slowly relaxed with the thought that all was well. The officers of King Ewald's castle respected Horst's judgment above any other. With a smile on his face, he watched the old innkeeper's wife rush toward them, her skirts flying about her aging legs.

Baron Otto

Lizelle was so excited by the thought of having both a Prince of Bavaria and a Princess of Austria in her inn she couldn't have been stopped had the entire armies of both kingdoms stood in front of her. Such was the fury of her excited rush, even the horses knew it was useless to stand in the way of this rapidly approaching lady. The horses moved aside, allowing Lizelle to approach the princess.

No one in the village of Nesterhoffen had ever seen anyone of more importance than a tax collector. As Lizelle neared the group of parting Austrian soldiers, she was overwhelmed by the realization of how incredible the events of this day were. But she understood that what she said, upon meeting the princess, would reflect not on her alone but on the entire village.

The nearer she came to the princess, the more she realized how important her mission was. Her enthusiasm was so great she could not slow her rushing feet, and she soon found herself standing between two horses – each carrying a beautiful princess.

Poor Lizelle's exhausted heart almost leaped from her gasping mouth as she realized there were not one but two princesses. Good Lord…Then, how many princes must there be? Lizelle's mind was swooning. Yet, with instincts only a woman understands or knows, Lizelle turned unerringly to the beautiful young daughter of the King of Salzburg and exclaimed, "Dear Princess Gotthardt, we of Nesterhoffen welcome you and are honored to have you here, especially arriving at the same time as Prince Von Nickolaus of Bavaria. May I offer you the hospitality of our inn? You may wish to rest and refresh yourself after your long ride."

Lizelle might have been talking to herself for all the attention anyone paid her after she mentioned the Prince of Bavaria.

The officers from Austria tried to appear nonchalant in their inspection of the Bavarian soldiers at the other end of the village. They whispered excitedly to each other, "I think he's the one on the far right." And then another said, "No… that must be him in the middle," which gave away their thrill at being so close to the next King of Bavaria.

None, however, was more thrilled than the two Princesses; though they both felt a sudden rush of color to their cheeks at being so bold, neither could restrain herself from rising slightly in her saddle to stare at the soldiers from Bavaria. As each soldier of the escort made a guess as to which the prince might be, the young girls' eyes switched excitedly to the soldier in question.

***

Prince Ludwig was oblivious to the events of the day. For him, this entire journey had been nothing but another way of passing through another dreary and meaningless day. Though a warm sun shone down on him, the singing of countless birds surrounded him, and the blossoms and fragrances of flowers beyond number assailed his eyes and nose, he noticed nothing but the regular, boring throb of his unavailing heart.

Now, his impatience at being left to sit in silent misery became more than he could bear. After hearing the annoying sounds of Arno's laughter as it drifted back to him from the center of Nesterhoffen, he pushed his horse forward through the ranks of his guard and proceeded toward Arno, a farm girl and a tall Austrian soldier, who were enjoying themselves immensely in the village square.

As Prince Ludwig's black stallion, Nightwind, came to a halt by Arno's and Horst's mounts, Arno recovered enough to introduce the prince to Horst and Gretchen and explain the situation. Arno assured his prince that the soldiers from Salzburg were only an escort for their princess. "Do not be concerned," he said, drawing himself as tall as possible; after all, this was the prince.

Now, young Prince Ludwig's attention was gained with a striking suddenness. He heard the approaching hooves of the group from Salzburg, and looking up, he gazed upon the most beautiful sight of all his eighteen long, boring years. There, riding toward him in the lead of her escort, was the stunningly beautiful young daughter of the King of Salzburg.

***

Princess Inga could not hide her impatience any longer. She said to no one in particular, "Yes, I think I'd like very much to freshen up at the inn." Prodding her horse forward, she led her group toward the center of Nesterhoffen, where another rider, sitting upon a large black stallion, had joined Horst, the farm girl, and the Bavarian soldier.

With her long black hair, shimmering and drifting about her shoulders and her clear green eyes bright with curiosity, she advanced upon the village square. The nearer she came to the tall, slender prince with his hair shining gold in the sun, his eyes the color of the deep blue sky, the more she knew that her dreams had finally been answered.

***

Mother Nature, seeing her handiwork in Nesterhoffen bloom, moved on. Hers was a busy world with many people and places in need of her blessings. But she could not help smiling to herself as she departed.

They make such a lovely young couple…thought Mother Nature.

29

Baron Otto

What the bees whisper to the flowers,

what the flowers whisper to the winds,

what a girl and a boy whisper to each other,

where love's sweet bloom begins.

Chapter V: Gay Confusion

It was a day of joyous confusion in Nesterhoffen.

Nine-year-old Gertrude Kruger raced from one house to the next, breathless and excited with the news. But as children are apt to do, when trying to explain something of great importance, the facts became very confusing due to her great excitement. By the time Trudy had told every villager her version of the news, most of them were completely befuddled.

Just like Oskar and Emma Claus who were working behind their small cottage in the vegetable garden, when little Trudy rushed up and said, "They're here! They're here! Oh! They're really here!"

"Calm down, little sparrow," said Oskar, rising from his garden.

"Emma," he admonished his wife with a playful grin, "Is this how you teach the village children to behave at school?"

Emma Claus was Nesterhoffen's unofficial school teacher. She gave Oskar a look to let him know she didn't appreciate his unkind remark and that he'd best hold his tongue, or he might find a wooden peg in his sauerkraut for supper. Then, Emma knelt before this child. "Now, now, Trudy," soothed Emma. "Who's here that's making you so excited?"

"The prince is here and a princess," stammered poor Trudy. "No, two princesses and an army of soldiers – or two armies, I think!" Trudy was breathless and confused. "Anyway, I think the king is coming too, maybe all the kings!" Trudy rattled on, "And I think they're in love!" Now Trudy blushed, for she was already in love with the golden prince who rode the beautiful black stallion; in fact, she hoped he wouldn't marry the dark-haired princess!

"Have you been drinking your father's beer? ... Oskar queried in a stern but amused tone. He couldn't make heads or tails of her story.

"Oskar Claus!" said Emma in a voice that she would brook no more of his barnyard humor, "Can't you see poor Trudy is almost in tears? She has something very important to tell us. Please be quiet and listen." Then, to Trudy, she said, "Now, slowly, child. What is all this talk about kings and princes and armies?"

"They're here!" repeated Trudy, wringing her hands. "They're all here at Herr Bauer's inn! And the prince is so handsome! He's riding on the biggest horse in the whole wide world, and I've got to go and tell my father in the hops field!" With that, young Trudy was off and running toward the hops field just as fast as her tiny feet could fly.

So, the villagers of Nesterhoffen came to learn, by one means or another, that an amazing event was taking place in their peaceful little village. Soon they all found an excuse to visit Herr Bauer's inn, hoping to catch a glimpse of the prince from Bavaria and the princess from Austria; though they paused long enough to put on their best Sunday clothes first.

Only those few who arrived within the first hour saw the prince and princesses at the inn. Prince Ludwig, upon discovering that Princess Inga had ridden along to Nesterhoffen to inspect the hops fields, suggested that since their missions were the same, perhaps she would be willing to join him so they could inspect the hops fields together.

Princess Inga agreed quickly, while Princess Eleanor found a sudden urge to look at the village from the other end of the town, leaving Ludwig and Inga with an outrageous wink of her eye.

Thus, for most of the afternoon, the young prince and princess could only be seen from a distance as they walked together inspecting the hops fields, the barley fields, the wheat fields, and strangely enough, fields that had nothing planted in them at all.

It was with a heavy heart that Princess Inga had to remind Prince Ludwig that the hour was growing late; she had to return to Salzburg, lest her father send out his army to find her. Prince Ludwig knew the truth of what she said, for his own father would do the same thing if he was late getting home.

When the two forlorn young people returned to Nesterhoffen, their sorrow at parting was plain to be seen by all. Though the prince and princess wanted with all their hearts to see each other again, neither knew how to go about it.

Fortunately, young Arno's quick mind found the solution. Just before the two groups said their farewells, he found the courage to say to Prince Ludwig, "Your Highness, perhaps it would be wise if we check these hops fields on a regular basis."

Everyone who had heard, which was everyone about, stopped to think about what he meant. But Horst, who was an excellent thinker himself, caught the meaning first and replied boldly, "I believe Herr Arno makes a good point, Your Grace.

I should think that the first day of each week would be proper... I mean, adequate for inspecting the hops fields."

By now, even the slowest minds among them had perceived the arrangements taking place, and Prince Ludwig and Princess Inga were not slow of mind. Their eyes met, and the glowing brightness between them would have lit the darkest room.

With a heart that was lit with newfound hope, Prince Ludwig said to all, though his eyes were only for Princess Inga, "I agree. And on such an important mission as inspecting these priceless hops fields, I think it only proper that I should come along."

Taking her cue, Princess Inga was quick to respond, "I agree, Horst. These fields are much too valuable not to be inspected on a regular basis. I'll speak to my father, King Ewald, and make sure that on the first sunny day of each week…when I'm sure, it won't rain, that we …someone rides to Nesterhoffen to inspect the hops fields."

Thus, the young couple, having made their arrangements to meet again in a proper if devious manner, parted with joyous hearts and cheerful goodbyes.

As Prince Ludwig rode out of Nesterhoffen, he was amazed by the beauty of this peaceful, little village. The hills seemed to be one vast carpet of brilliantly-colored and deliciously fragrant flowers. Everywhere he looked, a bird sang its melodious tune just for him. And how warm and gentle the sun shone here!

Such a truly wondrous and beautiful place! He sighed with satisfaction.

With the smile of my sigh

or the blush within my eye,

as a tear falls from my heart,

you will hear my soul shout love's cry,

for parting brings such sweet sorrow

and joys of gay confusion.

Chapter VI: A Homecoming to Bewilder Kings

If Princess Inga had been sullen and morose on her ride to Nesterhoffen, she was certainly not feeling dreary on her ride home to Salzburg. In fact, she was the gayest of the entire group. She bubbled with humor and good cheer … to the point of making everyone stop, while she happily picked a bright bouquet of flowers to take to her father. When one bouquet seemed too paltry a gift, she enlisted the aid of the others, and soon, all of them rode into the castle keep at Salzburg, singing a lyrical tune, each carrying a large, beautiful bouquet of flowers for King Ewald.

King Ewald was fretting in the courtyard and wondering miserably at the lateness of their return. Now, he was struck speechless at his daughter's sudden change of countenance and his soldiers carrying bouquets! To say that King Ewald was surprised by this scene would have been a dire misrepresentation of the truth.

King Ewald knew not whether he should rejoice or worry harder: certainly, all kings had a terrible penchant for worrying. Then, Princess Inga jumped down from her horse, ran to him, threw her arms about him in a mighty embrace and gave him a big kiss on the cheek.

"Oh, Father, I love you so much!" she gushed happily. Then she rushed into the castle, calling over her shoulder, "We've brought you some flowers. Come on, Eleanor, Horst. We've got to place the bouquets in vases of water!" She disappeared inside the castle where only her voice could be heard as she ran through the castle, gathering maids and servants to help her fetch vases for the flowers.

King Ewald's plan to make his daughter more cheerful had worked so well that he could only stroke at his beard furiously and wonder if it had been such a good idea, after all.

****

Prince Ludwig rushed back to his father's castle in Bavaria in such haste that Arno and the soldiers of his escort had barely a chance to exchange one word. So swift was the pace of the big black stallion upon which the prince rode that he arrived in the castle courtyard a good ten minutes before the others, to call out in great excitement, "Where's the Master-At-Arms? Has anyone seen the Master-At-Arms?"

King Karl, who had been waiting expectantly for his overdue child, thought his worst fears had been realized. The Austrian armies must have come through the pass and his son, "Bless him," thought King Karl, had raced ahead to warn him. King Karl hurried from his balcony to join Prince Ludwig in the courtyard, where the prince was explaining something vehemently to the Master-At-Arms.

"How many are there?" panted the pudgy little king, as he reached the young prince. "Are they far? Can Arno and the escort hold them off?

The prince responded with a puzzled expression on his face.

"The Austrian army!" shouted King Karl, grabbing his son and trying to shake some sensible answer loose. "How many … and how far away are they?" By now, the king's face was brilliantly red with frustration and anger.

"What Austrian army?" asked the hopelessly confused young prince.

"The one you've raced here to warn me about!" shouted King Karl.

"I didn't race here to warn you of any Austrian army, Father," replied a confused Prince Ludwig.

"You mean you raced in here with your horse in a lather, no escort in sight, hollering for the Master-At-Arms, exciting the whole palace, nearly giving me a stroke, and there's no army invading?" blubbered the King.

"I'm sorry if I excited you, Father, but the pass at Nesterhoffen is free of any troops." With a quick wink of his eye, the prince added, "The hops grow well!"

"Then why in the world were you shouting for the Master-At-Arms?" questioned the totally confused King of Bavaria, his eyes blinking back in nervous confusion.

"I … I … wanted to ask him if there was still time for me to take my swordsmanship lesson today," stammered the young prince.

"You what?" shouted the king, refusing to believe his own ears. "You raced in here raising an uproar throughout the castle … because you … want … to … OHHHH!" That was as far as the spluttering, sputtering king got before he turned and stumbled, slump-shouldered, back into his castle, muttering, "How miserable and unfortunate life has been to me! Why was I plagued with a son instead of blessed with a daughter?"

***

Within the span of one short day, Prince Ludwig had undergone a number of very drastic and remarkable changes. Since meeting the beautiful Princess Inga, he had made up his mind to excel in all things, hoping that if he became proficient enough, she would look upon him favorably.

And so, Prince Ludwig trained hard in the days ahead and studied late into the evenings with his father's best advisers, generals, scholars, swordsmen, falconers, horsemen, lancers, masons, grooms, mathematicians, and anyone else willing to teach him something.

Soon, anyone in the castle who knew anything at all walked softly when passing the young prince lest he spot them and drag them reluctantly into his chambers, where they would spend the rest of the day tutoring him.

On the first sunny day of each week, when he was sure it wouldn't rain, he put aside his books and weapons, had Arno form an escort, and rode to Nesterhoffen to inspect the hops fields.

****

Likewise, in the castle of King Ewald of Salzburg, Princess Inga was spending her hours in studies with her tutors and whispered, giggling conversations with her friend, Princess Eleanor. What would have shocked her father to the point of apoplexy had he known, was that Princess Inga had started secretly sewing her wedding gown after her very first visit to Nesterhoffen.

Princess Inga, though young, was a willful, strong-minded girl much like her father, and she had made up her mind to marry Prince Ludwig of Bavaria before they had departed the hops fields that very first day. So, on the first sunny day of each week, when she was sure it would not rain, she had Horst form an escort for her, and they rode to Nesterhoffen to inspect the hops fields.

The villagers of Nesterhoffen were quick to note that on the first sunny day of each week, the Prince of Bavaria and the Princess of Salzburg met in the village to check the hops fields together. So, on the first sunny day of each week, several village men cleared and mowed a pleasant place in a shady glade near a sparkling little brook. Meanwhile, the village women gathered at Herr Bauer's inn to help Lizelle prepare a picnic lunch for the young prince and princess. Thus, the pleasant months of spring and summer passed, but the young couple barely noted the coming and going of the seasons. Their hearts were sharing a different calendar and each moment they spent together was at once the longest second and the briefest hour.

Each loving gaze was an infinite time beyond measure. Yet, each day seemed to pass within the blink of an eyelash. Their love became like the blossoming of a flower, growing more complete and beautiful with each new breath of life, each new ray of sunshine.

For where is there in this enormous world a place?

And with exception only to our favorite dreams, a place,

so warm and comfortable with love

and our cherished things, a place,

somewhere we each call home

and fly to on breathless wings, a place,

that there each of us in life shall find

a homecoming to bewilder kings.

Chapter VII: A Problem Seen is a Problem Solved

As the harvest season drew near, the young lovers were faced with an almost insurmountable set of problems. Once the hops were harvested, the snows of winter would not be long in coming. With the snows would come the closing of the pass to Nesterhoffen and no longer would the kings worry until the following spring. For these reasons, the young prince and princess would not be able to see or communicate with one another until the following spring. More important, still, they had fallen deeply in love.

Each wanted desperately to marry the other, but neither of them could think of a likely way to approach their fathers with news of their love. One must remember that kings married children off as an arrangement of state and did not listen to any youthful declarations of love.

Princess Inga knew full well that her father was grooming her for an arranged marriage to a certain Prince Frederick of Vienna. Prince Ludwig was ashamed to admit to Inga that his father had mentioned a certain princess in Munich for him.

Try as they might, neither could think of a way to solve this dilemma. Both knew if they mentioned their love for each other to their fathers, their fathers would only see treachery and most likely prevent them from ever seeing one another again. In truth, such news could bring their two kingdoms to the brink of war, such being the temperamental and precarious imbalance of royal thinking.

Finally, Princess Inga decided to seek the advice of her father's trusted advisor, Horst. Likewise, Prince Ludwig sought advice and counseling from his best friend, Arno.

Soon, all four were sitting in the glade near the brook on the first sunny day of the week, at Nesterhoffen, where they discussed methods they might use to arrange the marriage.

"It would be so simple," said Arno, thinking aloud, "if only both kings weren't so afraid of being attacked by each other through this pass at Nesterhoffen. Why, I'll bet if they weren't so afraid of each other, they'd be great friends and think your marriage a wonderful idea!"

Though Prince Ludwig and Princess Inga could see his reasoning, they could only nod their heads in disconsolate agreement. Arno had stated the facts, but he certainly hadn't found a solution.

This simple truth, however, found fertile ground in the mind of Horst. He cleared his throat, "Harrrrumppp," to get the others attention. "I think what Arno said may be the solution," said Horst in his usual slow and thoughtful way.

The others waited in anticipation, especially Prince Ludwig and Arno. They had come to like Horst and admired his intelligence. "Since this pass at Nesterhoffen is such a worrisome problem to both kings," Horst went on, "wouldn't they both rest easier if there was a small castle with soldiers here to guard the pass?"

"My father would never allow the Austrians to build and fortify a castle at Nesterhoffen," Prince Ludwig said dismally.

"And my father would go to war before allowing the Bavarians to build an armed fortress here," added a disheartened Princess Inga.

"But what if only half of the troops were Austrian?" Horst said, a cunning smile spreading across his face.

The quick mind of Arno was first to catch the meaning; and his face broke into instant sunshine. "And the other half of the troops would be from Bavaria!" Arno added quickly.

Neither Prince Ludwig nor Princess Inga could see how a castle in Nesterhoffen with half Bavarian and half Austrian soldiers could help them. They only frowned at each other and shrugged their sad, weary shoulders.

Arno, grinning with a devilish luminance, said to Horst in a half-mocking manner, "And who do you think, of all the Bavarians you know, Horst, would be the one that your King Ewald might trust most?"

Horst, seeing the humor in Arno's method of allowing the lovers to know what both he and Arno were thinking, grinned back at Arno, saying, "I don't know, Arno." "He'd probably have to be someone pretty settled and honest. A married man, I should think."

By now, Princess Inga was suspicious. Never had she heard Horst play games with words, so she began to pay closer attention to what they were saying.

"And what person from Austria," the grinning Horst continued, do you think King Karl might trust in a castle at Nesterhoffen?"

"Oh, I should think much the same as King Ewald," Arno mused aloud, trying to suppress a grin and failing. "Someone who is honest, settled and from a good family and definitely married. In fact, she would probably have to be beautiful, too – like Princess Inga."

Suddenly, the pieces of the puzzle fell into place for Princess Inga. With a squeal of delight, she pounced first upon Horst, then Arno, to give them each a hug and a kiss on the cheek.

Poor Prince Ludwig had been lost in deep thought. Now, he stared in bewildered disbelief at the unexpected antics of his usually sensible true love.

Princess Inga turned to him and knelt before him on the grass. Her beautiful face shining joyfully, she took his hands in hers and teasingly said, "Would you mind so much living in a small castle in Nesterhoffen with me?"

It was a moment before Prince Ludwig had everything figured out. Then he, too, let out a boisterous cheer of delight. Gathering Princess Inga into his arms, he smothered her with kisses.

***

And so, their secret plan was made there in the peaceful glade by the sparkling brook at Nesterhoffen. Though the plan was good, there was still much to be done before it might be acceptable to Kings Karl and Ewald.

***

As Prince Ludwig rode back to his father's castle late that afternoon, he kept asking Arno, "But how do we get my father to agree to this?"

"Leave matters to me," Arno replied. "Just don't act too anxious when your father asks you to marry the daughter of King Ewald of Salzburg!"

Likewise, Princess Inga constantly badgered Horst with the same question as they rode home to Salzburg that afternoon: "But how will we get my father to agree?"

Horst replied: "Say nothing, Princess. And when your father asks you to marry the Prince of Bavaria, don't seem overly anxious."

Baron Otto

***

And so it came to pass that on almost the same hour of the same day, a wise and trusted advisor approached King Ewald of Salzburg, while another approached King Karl of Wasserburg. Both these wise men and trusted advisers placed a solution to the problem of the pass at Nesterhoffen before their king.

"If you could arrange a marriage between your kingdom and theirs," the adviser to King Karl whispered fervently, "and if each kingdom provided a modest amount of land on either side of the pass, and each helped equally to build a small but well-fortified castle at Nesterhoffen, and each provided a small but equal garrison of soldiers to guard the pass, why then you'd control the pass at Nesterhoffen!"

King Karl was confused. "But how does this allow me to control the pass at Nesterhoffen?"

"Why hasn't Prince Ludwig become one of the wisest and noblest of soldiers these past few months?" retorted the adviser. "And isn't he devoted to you and our kingdom in Bavaria? And does it not naturally follow that a Royal Prince from Bavaria would naturally rule his castle and, therefore, the pass?" The adviser to King Karl folded his arms across his chest and rested on his magnificent words of advice, words which he had inadvertently overheard while eavesdropping upon a couple of young officers of the guard in the stables that evening.

Finally, King Karl understood. "But, of course!" he exclaimed excitedly. "What a perfect solution!"

***

King Ewald of Salzburg was having an almost identical interview that evening. But in answer to King Ewald's question, "But how

46

would I control the pass at Nesterhoffen?" the answer was slightly different, for Horst was the one suggesting the arrangements to King Ewald.

"Your Highness," replied Horst in a confidential manner, "I have chanced to meet this young prince from Bavaria. He is a weak-minded and vacillating soldier. He's slow of wit and easily led by others. Princess Inga, as you well know, is a strong-minded young woman. She thinks quickly and clearly. Above all else, she is devoted to you and to Salzburg!"

"Yes, Yes, I see," replied King Ewald as he paced about his chambers and stroked his beard in contemplation. "I think you may have solved my problems."

"And, of course, Your Highness, I would be more than willing to offer my services in taking charge of our half of the garrison to watch over the situation for you," a hopeful Horst added. He had visions of Gretchen Kruger jumping about in his head.

"Yes. Oh, indeed, yes!" exclaimed the now excited king. "That would insure everything!"

Horst uncrossed his fingers from behind his back. The situation was definitely promising. Then King Ewald told him to send a messenger to King Karl of Wasserburg, saying that King Karl should expect a peaceful delegation from him on the following Sunday.

Thus, as things came about that Sunday, a procession of wise men, trusted advisers, two elderly aunts, pack horses carrying gifts, and a special envoy with a secret letter to King Karl, all escorted by Horst and eight officers, chanced to meet a procession of wise men, trusted advisers, two elderly uncles, pack horses carrying gifts, and a special envoy with a secret letter for King Ewald, all escorted by Arno and eight officers, while passing through Nesterhoffen.

Being sober and trusted officers on an important mission for their respective kings, Arno and Horst refrained from laughing aloud; they only smiled and winked at each other in passing. They were both delighted at how well their plan was working, though there still remained the decision of the kings.

For all things, there is a beginning and an ending.

For any question there will be an answer.

For as surely as night must follow day,

the solution will follow the question.

A problem that is clearly seen is a problem

whose solution is already foretold.

"A problem seen is a problem solved."

Chapter VIII: The Proposal of Kings

King Karl and King Ewald each received these worthy emissaries of wise men, trusted advisers, elderly aunts or uncles, and special couriers with sufficient pomp and ceremony as the importance of the occasion befitted.

That evening, in the castles of both kings, a large and festive banquet took place; the finest foods, wines, and entertainment were provided to the guests. As these festive banquets went on, one by one, the wise men, trusted advisers, uncles and aunts cornered the young prince or princess and questioned them. As the evening wore on, they gathered in twos and threes and compared information, finally forming an opinion as a group.

"Yes, he's weak and vacillating with a slow wit and should be easily led by Princess Inga," was the decision of the group at King Karl's banquet. Prince Ludwig had played his part well: he had, of course, been coached by Horst.

"She's certainly attractive enough and charming, but fortunately, she has little common sense and cannot think for herself," was the consensus of the group visiting King Ewald. Princess Inga was coached by Arno, and she played her role to perfection.

And so, the next morning before each procession took its departure, the special envoys delivered their secret letters from one king to the other. The two letters were as twins.

"To your Royal Highness, King Karl Wilhelm Von Nickolaus, King of Wasserburg:

"In that as much as your kingdom in Bavaria and my kingdom of Salzburg in Austria have both been friends and allies for many generations, I would like to suggest to you a way to show you my continued goodwill and strengthen our alliance further.

In that, I, King Ewald Herman Gotthardt of Salzburg, would deem a marriage between my one and only much-cherished daughter, Princess Inga Margret Gotthardt, and your fine and noble son, Prince Ludwig Johann Von Nickolaus, a match of highest honor.

And to further strengthen our alliance, if this marriage be acceptable to you, I propose that your kingdom and mine share equally in their marriage dowry, which I suggest should include:

1. The building of a small but adequate castle near the village of Nesterhoffen.

2. This castle to be built by an equal number of masons, architects, laborers, funds and materials from both our kingdoms.

3. A small but sufficient garrison of soldiers and officers to fortify the castle, made up of equal numbers from both our kingdoms.

4. An equal share of land to be given to the young couple to extend ten miles in any direction from Nesterhoffen. This to be theirs to rule over and tax as solely their domain.

5. A written pack of alliance from both our kingdoms to provide aid and succor, if our help should be needed.

Should you find this proposal to be acceptable, which I greatly hope, I will gladly accept your emissaries to help make all the arrangements.

If this proposal be not acceptable, I will receive your courier with the grace befitting his rank.

Your Ally and Friend, His Royal Highness
King Ewald Hermann Gotthardt, King of Salzburg"

Both King Karl and King Ewald must have been somewhat curious and confused by the fact that they both had thought of the exact same words to exchange at the exact time. But, since they were both kings, it was more or less to be expected. After all, it was an idea befitting a wise and brilliant king.

Rather than ponder over the strange duplication of circumstance, they merely attributed it to the other's good sense and fine judgment. Thus, their respect for each other grew immensely. Both kings stayed up all that night and into the next morning and afternoon with their wise men, trusted advisers, aunts or uncles, and decided the fate of their son or daughter.

***

The next day, Prince Ludwig of Bavaria practiced nervously with the Master-At-Arms in the castle courtyard, while his good friend Arno watched with amusement. He practiced with so much uncontrolled nervous energy that soon he had destroyed no less than three throwing lances, one shattering against a stone fountain no less than twenty yards from where he aimed. As for archery, his aim was no better. Though he shot twice as many arrows as the Master-At-Arms, he rarely hit a target. He became so ferocious during his swordsmanship lesson that the Master-At-Arms took his leave with a bloodied ear and refused to give him any more lessons for the day.

Indeed, the young prince was so nervous and impatient that after each cast of his lance or the flight of but two arrows, he would turn to ask Arno: "Do you think my father will agree? What could be taking so long? If he says, "No, I'll run away with Inga, and we'll live in the forest by ourselves." Without waiting for an answer, he dispatched yet another arrow or lance, only to watch it sail far over his target and shatter against the castle wall.

Arno only chuckled quietly to himself and stayed clear of the young prince.

Finally, in the late afternoon, while Arno sat on the stoop below the king's balcony watching the weary Prince Ludwig casting lances, King Karl appeared briefly on his balcony above and called out to his son, "Ludwig, I'd like to see you in my chambers for a moment." King Karl turned and walked back into his chambers, greatly worried about how he would get his son to accept this marriage graciously.

Prince Ludwig had been stopped in mid-cast; he gave a quick grin to Arno, then, threw his lance far and true to the heart of his target before rushing away.

Arno quickly caught up with him, cautioning, "Now remember, don't accept too hastily. Make him think you're doing this for him and Bavaria."

Young Prince Ludwig followed Arno's advice, and when he entered his father's chambers, he cast a meek and humble appearance as a good son should. "Yes, Father. You wanted to see me?" asked the prince, his heart racing with expectation.

"Ah, yes, Ludwig." The king's heart was also racing; he knew not how his son might react to what he was about to propose. "Come, Ludwig. Stand with me on the balcony. I have something of great importance I wish to discuss with you."

"Yes, Father," replied Prince Ludwig as he followed his father onto the balcony where they could see the courtyard below and off in the distant valley the faint outline of the city of Wasserburg and all the fields surrounding it.

Baron Otto

As the king stood leaning with his hands upon the balcony railing, he remarked to his son, "It's very beautiful, is it not, this kingdom in Bavaria?"

"Yes, Father," answered the impatient young prince: he wished his father would get to the point.

"Someday, this will all be yours," the king went on; his son's impatience went unnoticed. "Then, you will be king – and your son after you. But a king, whether it is I, or you after me, or your son after you, will always have many difficult decisions to make. In making any difficult decision, a king must always remember that the safety of his kingdom and its people must come before all else, even the king himself."

King Karl turned to watch his son's reaction to his speech.

"Yes, Father. I understand," replied Prince Ludwig; he really didn't understand at all. In fact, he was beginning to wonder if perhaps his father had decided against the marriage and was talking about something else.

"I have a very grave problem to solve, my son," said the pudgy little king as he reached up and placed an arm about his son. "And I'll need your help to solve it."

"If there is anything I can do to help, Father, you need only ask it of me," replied Prince Ludwig, thoroughly confused by his father.

"You have been a good son to me, Ludwig, especially in your concern and constant surveillance for the past few months of the pass at Nesterhoffen," went on King Karl. "You must realize by now how important that pass is to the safety of all Bavaria."

"Yes, Father. Whoever controls the pass at Nesterhoffen controls the entrance to Bavaria," said Prince Ludwig. With each mention of Nesterhoffen, he felt his excitement building.

"And you must know how fearful I've been these many years that a foreign army would move against us through that pass?" queried the king.

"Yes, Father. I share your concern," replied Prince Ludwig. "Certainly, there must be some way we can protect ourselves from that ever happening," said Prince Ludwig, hoping his words would lead his father to the conclusion he so desperately wanted.

"There is a solution, Ludwig. But it requires a great sacrifice on your part," said King Karl, searching his son's face for any signs of weakness or unwillingness.

"I will sacrifice even my life, Father, if that is what you require," replied Prince Ludwig.

King Karl was proud of his son for these words. A small tear formed in the corner of his eye, and with great difficulty, he said, "Then, I offer you this proposition, my son, for the good of Bavaria and the safety of all its fine people." The king crossed his fingers behind his back for luck and cleared his throat nervously. "Would you consent to marry the daughter of King Gotthardt of Austria?"

Young Prince Ludwig uncrossed the fingers he had held behind his back and turned away from his father to sigh in relief and happiness. When he regained his composure, he turned to his father. "If this would in some way help to protect Bavaria, Father, I would consider it an honor," said Prince Ludwig with all the seriousness he could muster.

Now, it was King Karl's turn to let out a sigh of relief and uncross his pudgy fingers. Clasping his son in a great hug of affection, he said, "My son, my noble son, you make me very proud this day!" Grasping the prince by the arm, he pulled him excitedly back into his chambers and began to explain.

He and King Gotthardt would build them a fine little castle at Nesterhoffen. This would protect the pass for both Bavaria and Austria. It would be built and garrisoned by equal numbers of workers and soldiers from both kingdoms. And on and on rambled the joyous king while Prince Ludwig was most impatient to leave and report the good news to his friend Arno, who waited on the other side of the chambers' door.

Finally, as King Karl's excitement waned and Prince Ludwig's reached a point near bursting, the king let him go with a final, "You've made me very proud, Ludwig!"

Prince Ludwig was already halfway out into the hallway and had been grabbed by the arm by an extremely curious and impatient Arno. Over his shoulder, he hastily replied, "Yes, Father! Thank you, Father!"

A moment or two later, King Karl was surveying his now empty chambers with a pleased and proud expression on his face when he heard a loud, raucous commotion somewhere out in his hallway. "Now, what in the world could that be all about?" he exclaimed, puzzled.

***

In the castle of King Ewald of Salzburg, a very nervous king paced back and forth in his private chambers. Stroking his beard in contemplation, he paused often in mid-stride to practice his prepared speech on an empty chair in the center of the room.

When he was finally ready, he straightened his shoulders and, with a purposeful stride, marched to his chamber door and flung it open. Looking about the corridor, he spied a castle maid busily dusting objects with no dust on them. Calling her over, he bid her find Princess Inga at once and send her to him immediately.

No sooner had King Ewald reentered his chambers and closed the door behind him, than the young maid lifted her skirts and ran like the wind down the hallway to skid to a halt in the middle of the next crossing corridor. Whispering in a hoarse and excited voice that was loud enough to carry throughout most of the castle and quite plain for another maid to hear forty feet away – one who stood dusting yet more dustless objects – she called, "Pssssst, Marie."

Marie turned quickly upon hearing her name and saw the first maid waving and psssting furiously at her. "Now?" whispered Marie excitedly back at the first maid.

"Yes! Now!" hollered the first maid in her best imitation of a whisper.

Marie hoisted her skirts and ran down yet another hallway that ended with a skidding stop at the next connecting corridor. Forty feet away was yet another dusting maid, and the process was repeated.

And on the message flew, down hallways and up staircases, through the corridors and across passageways within the castle, until Princess Eleanor rushed breathlessly into Princess Inga's bed chamber.

Baron Otto

There, the beautiful young Inga paced nervously to and fro, stroking her smooth and rounded chin. "Now?" queried Princess Inga even before Princess Eleanor could regain breath enough to speak. Poor, exhausted Princess Eleanor could only nod.

Princess Inga, not one to waste time in small conversation on such a momentous occasion, flew from her bed chamber and down the corridors, her skirts gathered high in both hands. When she raced by one of the maids, the maid would curtsy politely. And as soon as the young princess had zoomed by her, the maid would jump up with a broad smile on her face and join the growing group of charging ladies racing along in Princess Inga's wake.

Soon, a goodly number of maids, handmaidens, cousins, and ladies-in-waiting, who, judging by their pace, were waiting no longer, were flying towards the King's chambers.

Young Princess Inga reached the door to King Ewald's chambers almost before he had sent for her, so efficient had Princess Eleanor's inventive arrangements been with the maids. Princess Inga was in such a high state of excitement she forgot all about the words of caution that Horst had counseled. After all, this was the most important moment of her young life!

Rushing into the king's chambers and finding him posed sternly by the great fireplace beneath the flag of Salzburg, she ran to him and embraced him, tears of joy coursing down her flushed cheeks.

As she hugged and kissed her totally confused father, she made him forget his well-planned speech.

Never mind…she was prepared. "Oh, yes, Father. I'll gladly marry Prince Ludwig. And we'll make you so happy! We'll guard the pass for you, and you'll never have to worry again. And, Oh, Father, we'll be so happy in Nesterhoffen. Eleanor can come to visit me," and on and on. Then, Princess Inga led her totally bewildered father about by the arm, explaining where she wanted the castle built and how the different rooms were to be placed.

Poor King Ewald could only walk along with her in silent disbelief and wonder why all the maids were gathered around outside his open chamber door, grinning like a bunch of happy geese.

Why was I not blessed with a sensible boy child? – thought King Ewald, as he felt the first pangs of a headache coming on.

Baron Otto

There comes in the life

of every man and woman

that one special day for deciding.

Deciding upon which path the

relationship of love must travel.

May they all choose wisely and

always remain true.

Chapter IX: Marriage

The marriage between Prince Ludwig and Princess Inga was finally arranged. The date decided upon by the kings was to be the first Sunday in September of the following year. This would give the workmen at the new castle in Nesterhoffen sufficient time to build reasonable living quarters for the young couple and their servants.

The wedding would take place at the castle of King Ewald of Salzburg. The entire week before the wedding would be spent in various festivities. Invitations were sent by special messengers to nobility near and far, and all the villages of both kingdoms were invited to send a small delegation.

Meanwhile, the kings lost no time in assigning their best craftsmen and laborers to the new castle in Nesterhoffen. Great amounts of lumber and stone were freighted daily to the small village throughout the remaining days of summer and fall, so that the construction of the castle might proceed throughout the winter months. Though it was expected to take six years or more to complete the castle, at least it would be sufficiently completed by the following year's September to allow the newlyweds to live in reasonable comfort.

As things went well on the one hand, they did not go so smoothly on the other. Once King Karl and King Ewald had agreed to the marriage, neither king would allow their children to meet prior to the wedding. Both kings reasoned unknowingly that if their son or daughter should meet their betrothed beforehand and not like what they found, they might become overly passionate in their refusal to go through with the marriage.

Meanwhile, Prince Ludwig and Princess Inga could not speak the truth to their fathers. For such was the imperfect balance and acute temperament of the rulers. A simple confession of truth to one or the other of them might very well start a chain reaction of punishments that could easily ruin their marriage and even hurt the poor villages of Nesterhoffen, to say nothing of wars and general devastation. So, everyone waited out the dreary months until the wedding.

Both kings did, however, allow the prince and princess to write to each other, though to be sure, each letter was carefully monitored; nothing written should upset the forthcoming union. This kept young Arno and Horst very busy indeed. Throughout the late summer and fall, they scurried back and forth between the castles, delivering multitudes of letters written by the young couple.

Of course, these letters were always handed directly to either King Karl or King Ewald to read first before they were given to Prince Ludwig or Princess Inga. Therefore, the letters were written in a very circumspect and general manner, having much to do with the weather conditions and general discourse as to hobbies and crafts they enjoyed.

Horst and Arno, however, always made a stop at Herr Bauer's inn when passing through Nesterhoffen to deliver their mail. There, they would entrust to Lizelle a very different type of letter. When Horst and Arno passed through Nesterhoffen on their return home, Lizelle gave them these secret letters for their prince or princess. These letters were delivered secretly to the young prince and princess; letters, you may be assured, that said nothing at all of the weather conditions or hobbies but spoke of love's burning flame and eternal devotion.

But soon, the letters stopped, for the snows of late fall had closed the pass for the winter. Everyone concerned was left to wait out the winter in their private misery. All that is, except Arno and Horst, who got a much needed rest.

***

As all things pass with time, so, too, did the winter. The warm spring melted the winter snow and made the pass usable once again. Both Horst and Arno were set to carrying letters at an enormous rate, for Princess Inga and Prince Ludwig had written two sets of letters apiece each day throughout the winter and had accumulated quite a large stockpile.

Both King Karl and King Ewald could only wonder at this vast quantity of mail that said nothing of significance. Yet, their offspring seemed to take such great delight in reading daily tales of last winter's weather reports that neither king was inclined to say anything, fearful their child might realize what a dull marriage was in the making.

Finally, toward the end of August, as the wedding drew near, the castle at Salzburg took on a festive appearance. Royalty from all corners of Europe began to arrive for the wedding. No one was more welcome than Princess Eleanor of Vienna, who was to be Princess Inga's handmaiden.

Many were the hours these two beautiful, young princesses spent locked in Princess Inga's room, giggling and crying, laughing and sighing, as Princess Inga read her private love letters to her best friend and sought her advice.

The most impressive procession by far arrived exactly one week before the wedding. This was the procession from the lands of Germany that had gathered at the castle of King Karl of Wasserburg. No fewer than ten other German kings had come in person or sent emissaries of high noble rank. There were dozens of dukes and earls, scores of distinguished knights and clergymen, princes and princesses. Each entourage brought with them many servants, soldiers and athletes; falconers, wrestlers and strongmen; jugglers and musicians; horsemen, buffoons and dandies; archers, astrologers and craftsmen of all pedigree and manner. The procession seemed almost endless.

Behind this noble entourage, led by King Karl and Prince Ludwig, came the delegations from more than forty villages of Bavaria, led by the delegation from Nesterhoffen, Herr Bauer at its head.

Soon, the entire valley surrounding King Ewald's castle at Salzburg was covered with tents and banners of all descriptions and colors, and people of all manner of dress and speech, wandering gaily about, laughing and enjoying each other's company.

Princess Inga, who stood at the highest turret of her father's castle, enjoyed none of this wild and wonderful spectacle. Her eyes were for only one distant figure amid the vast multitudes: Prince Ludwig.

Soon, the premarital games commenced. Each sport was announced throughout the valley by a gaily-clad herald on horseback who rode through each encampment to announce the location of each event.

The wagering on these events was almost as reckless as the participants who gave their all to win. Horses, lands, money, clothes, jewelry, anything and everything might ride on the outcome of a wrestling match or flight of a single arrow.

These joyous and wondrous days passed in a confusion of gay abandonment and chivalry, until only one day remained before the marriage ceremony. This was the day everyone had waited for. This was the day of the final event and the awards feast.

The final event was to test the best horse and horseman. Not only those that were gathered at Salzburg would be keenly interested, but all of Europe and lands as far as the word could spread would listen with rapt attention to its outcome.

Eleven countries would compete, twenty-seven kingdoms in all. Thirty-five lesser noblemen had entries. Close to one hundred of the finest horses and riders in Europe were to compete.

Three courses were set up throughout the valley. The first course was a sprint. The second course contained obstacles and jumps. The third and final course was a grueling three miles that would test both horse and rider to their maximum capability.

Only the best horse from each of the qualifying rounds of horses could advance to the next race, until only twelve horses remained to run the final grueling course. Only the winner of that final race would claim victory. Only one could be called the champion.

The betting was fierce and grew wilder with each preliminary race. The ranks of those who had come for the wedding festivities became swollen by hundreds more who came just for the horse races. The valley was a pandemonium of screeching, cheering madness. As difficult as it was to tell one person from another in this swirling mass of spectators, it was doubly so for the spectators who could only glimpse for a moment or two a flashing horse and rider. But, one horse and rider did stand out.

This was a rider dressed in black, red, and green, who rode upon a magnificent black stallion. He was a blond young man from

Bavaria, a prince by the name of Ludwig Johan Von Nickolaus. For this was his time. And the day before his wedding was also his day to shine.

In a feat of almost insurmountable odds and endurance, in tests of skill and courage, in race after race and trial after trial, Ludwig overcame the best that could be sent against him. And finally, his magnificent black stallion, Nightwind, pulled him into the lead to win the final race and the championship. The cheers that resounded throughout the valley at Salzburg could be heard for miles in every direction. And the cheering of two particular kings and one particular princess were the loudest of all.

***

The wedding day dawned clear and bright. Even the fluffy white clouds that drifted lazily overhead seemed dressed for the occasion. Wherever one looked, one saw men and women, boys and girls, even horses and their grooms decked out in their finest, most colorful clothing, each person and animal, an eye-catching attraction of every conceivable color and style.

If some had not won an award for skill at the games, they could have won a prize for the most entrancingly dressed. Yet, as handsome as the men were, they were no match for the ladies.

Of all the ladies, two stood out from the rest: Princess Eleanor, beautiful in her gown of blue and gold, and the exquisite Princess Inga, wearing a pure white gown with emerald green and rose-pink trim. They shone as two jewels among a gathering of pebbles.

Though the service was long and official to the point of being stuffy (for, at times, it seemed more like two kingdoms being wed instead of two people), Prince Ludwig and Princess Inga seemed not to mind at all. At long last, as the bishop intoned his final blessing upon them, Ludwig could not help being so swayed by the tears that softly glided over Inga's lovely cheeks, that he did not notice his own. Then, the bishop intoned, "I now pronounce you man and wife," With these words, a tremendous cheer and clanging of bells erupted from inside the castle. The clamor soon passed like a tidal wave to those waiting outside the castle. It spread like a bolt of lightning and crash of thunder past the castle gates and through the valley camps.

Little Gertrude Kruger was far back in the valley with her small group from Nesterhoffen, sitting perched on a low tree branch she was one of the last to know. When the cheering finally reached them and all knew that the prince and princess were wed, little Trudy did no cheer. The tears that ran down her soft, tender cheeks were not from happiness but the agony of heartbreak and despair. Little Trudy had lost her prince.

Baron Otto

For marriage is like the joining of two waves at

sea. Two waves that meet in mid-ocean,

that fall in love, and unite as one.

That travel through the despair and heartbreak

of one storm after another, both great and small.

And, as some waves can be broken apart by the

merest thunder shower,

yet others can be broken apart by nothing at all.

No typhoon, no hurricane, no tempest, nor

tragedy of each can rend them asunder.

And at life's final, last fleeting moment, they will

gently roll upon a soft and gentle shore and

there to rest in their shared

tranquility… forever more.

Chapter X: The Castle and the Carpenter

So, it came to pass that a great joy encompassed all who lived in Nesterhoffen, for the prince and princess were of good heart and gentle disposition. So abundant was their love for each other that it spilled over to enfold all those who lived in Nesterhoffen. They were as neighbors to good friends, not masters to vassals.

The work on the small castle was being done with exceptional speed and efficiency; Horst and Arno worked well together and organized the laborers so that no time was lost in wasted effort. At least, that is, whenever King Ewald and King Karl were not underfoot.

If the truth be known, both kings had come to be very fond of their new son-in-law and daughter-in-law and were prone to visit Nesterhoffen at the slightest excuse. Not that Ludwig or Inga minded these frequent, unexpected visits: both of them were also growing fond of their new fathers-in- law.

To Arno and Horst, however, these visits by the kings were a great nuisance. Well-laid and efficient plans to build the castle suddenly unraveled at the seams when the kings were on hand, for kings have a penchant for doing things in their own way, each one thinking his way is the best way. No matter the consequences or lack of proficiency in what they tried, inevitably, they did it their way....anyway.

Thus, when both kings arrived in Nesterhoffen, all too soon, they were seen marshaling the respective forces from their own kingdoms and instructing them on how their half of the castle was to be built.

If these two noble monarchs had been left to their ways long enough, the castle at Nesterhoffen would have taken twice as long to build and would have had two halves that did not fit together.

Fortunately, their visits were not overly long or frequent. The snows of fall came early that year. Unlike the winter before, they were welcomed by all in Nesterhoffen for reasons each to his own.

Arno, now, a captain in charge of the Bavarian contingent, sighed in blissful relief and relaxed his pace from the hectic endeavors of the past few months. While Horst, who was a captain in charge of the Austrian contingent, suddenly found a boundless new energy that kept him constantly busy, running between his official duties at the castle and his unofficial duties at the Kruger farmhouse. The young prince and princess found those few moments of solitude together to begin building cherished memories.

Most of all, the slowing of the frenzied pace of the castle's construction was welcomed by the workers and laymen themselves. Though most of them returned to their respective castles in Salzburg or Wasserburg, a few remained behind to continue with work they could do throughout the winter. A great many trees were felled and prepared at Nesterhoffen during the winter months, and a tremendous amount of woodwork and carpentry skills were required to finish and furnish the inside of the castle.

For these reasons, a certain village carpenter of Nesterhoffen, Oskar Claus, became known to Horst and Arno. Oskar Claus was not only an exceptionally fine carpenter, but he also knew well the nearby forest where the choicest prime trees of different types grew and how to season the wood for carpentry use. Oskar Claus was much in demand by Horst and Arno for his skills and expertise.

Emma Claus was busier still. The winter months were always busy months for her as the unofficial schoolteacher of the village children. Many were the lessons the village children learned as she told tales from the Bible each winter. But what made Emma busier still were her skills at cooking. The workers from Salzburg and Wasserburg who remained in Nesterhoffen for the winter discovered that Emma Claus was by far the best cook in Nesterhoffen and most probably in much of Bavaria and Austria as well. The lines of craftsmen working on the castle at Nesterhoffen that winter were exceptionally long at the Claus's small log house at breakfast, lunch and dinnertimes. Each craftsman had some seemingly unsolvable problem for Oskar and a hopeful, hungry glint in his eye. Oskar and Emma saw to their problems and their hunger. No place on earth was more caring for the needs of strangers than this small log house of Oskar and Emma Claus.

So their names, spoken with love, grew just as the castle, slowly, among a chosen few. They were as the heart of the village itself and each village like it throughout the world.

Baron Otto

Nature has a need for all things on earth, and all

things have a purpose.

We are but a single thing in nature's plan, yet

she favors us with a great purpose.

For we are the carpenters of her castle.

Let us build it slowly, together, and with great love.

PART 2: THE TOYMAKER

FIVE YEARS HAVE PASSED

Chapter I: A Man in Need

Five years passed before Mother Nature returned to check upon her handiwork at Nesterhoffen. She was filled with contentment and joy at what she had wrought. The village of Nesterhoffen was blossoming as her most precious and delicate mountain flower.

Where once the mountain pass had been used by none but the hops growers from Nesterhoffen going to sell their wares in Salzburg and Wasserburg, now it was used by merchants from all the surrounding kingdoms and nations. They crossed through Nesterhoffen to buy and sell their different wares, and many were the busy merchants among them who were so astonished at the beauty and friendliness of the place that they stayed an extra day or two or three or more.

The prince and princess decided not to overly tax these merchants as most other kingdoms did. In fact, only a one- pfennig toll per person was charged to use the pass. This was so inexpensive and reasonable to the merchants that many traveled far out of their way to use the pass at Nesterhoffen. As each merchant crossed the newly-built bridge over the sparkling stream at Nesterhoffen, an officer of the guard collected the one-pfennig tax. In truth, one could not pass through Nesterhoffen without crossing this bridge. Thus, the village at Nesterhoffen became a busy and bustling place.

Throughout the spring, summer and fall, a veritable army of merchants swept through Nesterhoffen, going to and coming from the various capitals and places of note throughout Europe. Not a few stopped long enough at the growing village of Nesterhoffen to do a bit of trading there. Such was the prosperity of those who tarried in Nesterhoffen that many of them decided to return the next year.

Among them was a poor, elderly Jewish merchant from Vienna, by the name of Ishman.

Poorly clothed and mostly impoverished, Ishman had hardly any goods to trade worth mentioning: his single broken-down old cart with worthless junk was pulled by a half-lame, even older, donkey.

As poorly as the old peddler appeared on the outside, he was twice as rich as King Solomon on the inside. For Ishman lived and breathed for great ideals. While his Jewish compatriots were penned up each night behind a locked gate in a small section of Vienna, he traveled freely throughout the countries and kingdoms of Europe. Oh, not richly by any means, and certainly with more restrictions placed upon him than on the other gentile traders and merchants. But there were no locked gates each night; no walls or guards surrounded him as he slept. Only the forests and stars above were his companions.

For these few comforts of freedom, Ishman was content, since his great and noble ideals were of freedom: freedom to travel where he desired, to trade with whom he chose, to speak his mind freely, to choose the religion that most comforted him and, to select his friends for the sake of their friendship alone; not for some secret gain sake of influence, power or wealth.

As it happened, the old peddler Ishman passed through the tiny village of Nesterhoffen, and his cart broke down. It was as if providence had guided his way; his humble, broken cart rested in front of the door to Oskar and Emma Claus' small log house at lunchtime.

Already a half-dozen workers from the castle were gathering by the Claus' front door. But, none went to the aid of the poor Jew, Ishman, with his broken cart and weary, half-lame donkey. Each of them was content to stand by the front door to Oskar and Emma's house and smell the fragrant aromas of Emma's cooking. The only attention they paid the old man while he struggled with his broken cart, was to cast snide remarks and make ribald jokes at his expense. Then, Oskar Claus came walking up from his morning's labors at the castle and noticed what was happening.

When the half-dozen raced to greet him, in hopes of being asked to lunch, Oskar asked them one question: "Why do you stand in front of my door with nothing to do, and yet, none of you turn a hand to help this poor old man?"

Their replies were a garbled collection of indignant shouts. "But he's just a Jew," yelled one.

"A peasant peddler and probably a cheat," cried another.

"A sack of fleas to nest in more than anything," cried another.

And even less complimentary remarks about poor old Ishman, his broken cart, and half-lame donkey followed.

Oskar Claus was taken aback and bewildered by these men with whom he'd worked for so long. They were not as he thought them to be. But, then, Oskar had never before seen or heard of a Jew. This posed a mystery to him. Were Jews like the dwarfs, pawns of the devil, mistrusted and treated as witches' consorts? Not that Oskar Claus knew much of these things either, but witches and their pawns, the dwarfs who lived deep in the forests; of them, he'd certainly been warned.

Yet, this poor old fellow who labored so futilely with his broken-down cart certainly appeared no more than what he seemed. Oskar was unsure of what he should do, especially as his acquaintances from work were now entreating him to forget the worthless old man and help them solve their problems, especially their gnawing hunger.

Oskar was not to be put off so easily. He waved them into silence and approached the old man. "Old man," he said, "can I help you?"

Old Ishman stopped his useless ministrations to the broken cart and raised himself as straight as his tired, weary body could go. Looking straight into the eyes of Oskar Claus and down into this very soul, Ishman saw neither another heckler nor antagonist but a kindred spirit. "I'm afraid, my good fellow, that neither of us can help," he said in a mellow, fatherly way. "The axle is completely broken. Neither of us can fix that. Anyway, I would be unable to pay for a new one in any case."

Oskar not only bent to look, for he had read into the eyes of Ishman as well, but stretched out on his back in the dirt and crawled under the cart to judge its damage. Assessing the problem, he crawled back out, stood up and said to the hapless stranger, "My name is Oskar Claus, and this is my home, which I share with my wife, Emma. I think I can fix your cart. Would you care to join my wife and me for lunch and discuss it?" With that, he offered a handshake to the bewildered old man and Ishman became a friend to the village carpenter.

The Claus home had but one guest for lunch that day. In the afternoon, Oskar built a new axle for Ishman's cart and repaired it, refusing all compensation. After all, Ishman was a stranger in need and their guest. When Ishman departed with the gift of a small wooden toy carving, which he had admired greatly, their friendship was a firm one.

Baron Otto

As ships that passed in the night, the two had met and parted. Both were strangers to each other in all things and without any understanding of each other's deeper meanings, but they had found a common ground – the faith and fellowship of human kindness.

It was a fragile and tentative bond, to be sure. Yet, it was one that would weld these two men together unto the ages and all of mankind forever.

No matter what position, wealth or influence,

no matter what your upbringing or your seed,

yet undaunted, we must join to fix the cart,

and help it to proceed.

For we have but one cart and no replacements,

…earth…and we must do greatness together

or fail in our deed!

Chapter II: The Chapel on the Hill

The village of Nesterhoffen grew and prospered. The fields and animals flourished, and the peasants grew fat. Where once they had known no outsiders, now they were like leaves upon a tree, each differently colored and shaped, yet with a fat and ready purse. The simple peasants of Nesterhoffen were quick at learning to scent out the jingling fat purses and relieve the merchant traders of some of the weight.

As the castle grew, so did the village's greed. None was spared this sickness, not even the prince and princess. Soon, the toll bridge at Nesterhoffen was charging two pfennigs, then three pfennigs, then four pfennigs for each person and one pfennig for each horse, ox or donkey.

Where a few years ago Herr Bauer traded a liter of beer or dinner or a room for the night for a goose egg, half a bale of hay, or a small piglet, now he charged three pfennigs for a beer, five pfennigs for food, and five pfennigs for a night's stay in one of his three dilapidated rooms upstairs.

Almost all of those in Nesterhoffen were touched by greed. Yet, two of the villagers did not succumb – Oskar and Emma Claus, who had no greed in their hearts, only kindness.

Oskar and Emma watched as their friends and neighbors lost their reason and common sense. The children were taught by their parents and came to Emma's schooling no longer. No more did they hear Emma's stories from the Bible. No more did they eat her freshly baked cookies. No more did they see and play with Oskar Claus' carved wooden toys. The children became miniatures of their parents and thrived on the barter and sales of even their own pets.

As all things flourished in Nesterhoffen, it came as no great surprise to anyone when the prince and princess announced the expectancy of a child. Four weeks of rejoicing were declared for all, with all tolls and charges by the royal couple's decree, being exempt. Joyous was the feasting and partying that October in that long ago year.

The noblest of all gestures by the prince and princess was to proclaim the month of October an open holiday period for Nesterhoffen. Each Friday of the month was given over to their hearing of petitions from peasants, villagers, merchants, travelers, and tradesmen. Their decisions to these petitions were just and fair, as in the petition of Herr Kruger, who had lost two of his geese to a runaway hay cart belonging to one of his neighbors, Jahnu Betcher.

It seems that Jahnu's twelve-year-old son was delivering some hay and had not tied the horse pulling the hay cart while he unloaded the cart. Some disturbance had frightened the animal, and it bolted down the main street of Nesterhoffen, pulling the unmanned and wildly swinging hay cart in its wake.

Fortunately, everyone had dodged out of its way to safety; everyone, that is, but two of the four geese that young Trudy Kruger was herding over to Herr Bauer's inn to deliver. These two geese were crushed by the overturning cart.

Herr Kruger was petitioning for the twenty pfennigs the lost geese were to bring upon their delivery to Otto Bauer's inn. Jahnu Betcher maintained that it was only an accident and that never before had anyone paid such an outrageous price for two miserable, scrawny geese.

The prince and princess reached their decision after first learning from Otto Bauer that he had, indeed, agreed to pay twenty pfennig for the two geese.

"Herr Betcher," the prince proclaimed, "the price of the geese was agreed to and was forfeited by the carelessness of your son. For this, you must pay Herr Kruger twenty pfennigs in coin or trade."

Princess Inga also pronounced justice in the matter. "That you might know the value of Herr Kruger's geese in the future. Herr Kruger will have you and your family over to dinner at his house the next time they cook a goose." She continued before the sputtering protests of Herr Kruger could interrupt. "And, as your son was as much at fault in this matter and young Trudy might have been run over instead of the geese, I think it would be to everyone's future benefit that your son place a number of hitching posts throughout Nesterhoffen."

Thus, was the justice of the petitioners performed. Most of the petitions were small grievances and petty matters. But one petition that October stood out from all the rest, for it was the petition of Oskar and Emma Claus. Their petition did not concern a mere misunderstanding with a neighbor or a simple accident. Oskar and Emma Claus were petitioning the prince and princess to be allowed to build a small chapel in Nesterhoffen.

Such was the temperament and misunderstanding of the religion of those times that a great hush fell over those present. Many nations and kingdoms were at war because of their differences in religion.

The prince and princess counseled with their most trusted advisers over the matter. Finally, after much arguing among themselves, they gave their decision.

"A small chapel building is admissible on the following conditions," stated Prince Ludwig. "Firstly, it must be built outside the village of Nesterhoffen and away from the main road so it will not be an angry eyesore to foreign merchants who hold other beliefs."

"Secondly," he continued, "all labor and costs of the building must come from those who wish it built." Here, the prince paused to make his point stronger; "And none who works on the castle will be excused from his work for this chapel building. Any who wish to work on the chapel must do so on their own time. The villagers will have no outside priest but must hold service by themselves."

Since everyone in Nesterhoffen was busy working at the castle from sunrise each morning to sunset each evening, the young royal couple and their counselors were convinced that this would be the end of the matter.

But Oskar and Emma Claus were of a different mind. They had seen their friends and neighbors grow as strangers to each other. Many were losing the simple but honest faith they had held in each other. Emma and Oskar were determined to bring them back together, much as a shepherd whose flock has been scattered by a sudden storm.

They chose a place on a small hill near the prince and princess' old picnic glade. Each night, after their work on the castle was done, they walked to the small hill on the outskirts of Nesterhoffen to clear the ground for the laying of a foundation.

For many nights, they worked alone, and their progress was painfully slow. When their neighbors finally stopped laughing at this immense task that the Clauses had set for themselves, they realized that what Oskar and Emma were doing each night was not hopeless or futile, not a self-serving endeavor, but a self-sacrificing attempt to reunite the villagers themselves. Slowly, their awareness grew to understanding.

By one's and two's, and finally whole families together, the villagers met on the hill by the blade each night. Weary from their day's labor, they found unbelievable new energy through the companionship of their neighbors. Here was a task worth doing!

Without a person being asked, they provided; without a hat being passed, they gave their time, their money, what materials or labor was needed. Soon, the village of Nesterhoffen became united again. Upon placing the first stone of the foundation, they named it: "The Chapel of Good Fellowship."

85

For the placing of but one stone, if it is the right stone

and the right place, makes a memorial throughout ages.

But as the stone must also have a heart and a soul,

and in its time, must laugh and cry.

We should treat it with a deference as someday

the stone may be you or I.

And as for myself, in such circumstances,

place me near the chapel on a hill.

Chapter III: The Shadow of One Man's Will

The prince was much concerned by the doings of Oskar and Emma Claus, and the building of their small chapel on the hill. Neither Prince Ludwig nor Princess Inga nor any of their wisest advisers had conceived of the people seriously going ahead with this undertaking. To some degree, the prince became jealous of the Clauses.

These people seemed to achieve more work in a few hours of torch-lit darkness on their charitable work than he received from a vaster gathering of paid workers for longer hours during daylight. The unfairness of this situation didn't suit him.

What worried him most of all was the garrulous grumbling he'd heard from the passing noblemen who stopped on occasion at the castle of Nesterhoffen. Many of these noblemen were bound for religious wars to fight and die for their beliefs in God. The people they went to slay in the name of their God were guilty of nothing more than choosing to worship God in a different manner and custom. For such narrow, single-mindedness, they set out to slay tens of thousands of one another and rejoice in the doing. The seeds of hatred and death they would sow would last for centuries, and for centuries, they would reap the sour fruit of this seed – hatred, death, and destruction.

The Prince of Nesterhoffen was greatly worried by the garrulous nature of these crusaders, who viewed the slowly rising chapel on the hill at Nesterhoffen as an affront to their way of worship. For the small chapel had no official sanction from their church and was thus considered a blasphemy in their eyes.

Prince Ludwig decided to stop the building of the chapel at once before a large contingent of crusaders passed through Nesterhoffen and burned his village with their religious zeal; for many years would pass before the High Bishop of Vienna could come to sanction the chapel.

Prince Ludwig summoned the village elder, Herr Bauer to his castle and bade him bring Oskar Claus along as well.

When they had been ushered into his presence, he spoke to them in a stern, yet fatherly manner, saying, "Herr Bauer and Herr Claus, I have called you here to tell you of the problems your little chapel is causing. First of all, most of the villagers work on my castle by day, and for this, I pay by cutting your taxes in half and exempting you from all the tolls and duties. Is this not so?"

"Yes, your Highness," chorused the two men of Nesterhoffen.

"And is that not a good bargain for the villagers of Nesterhoffen?" queried Prince Ludwig.

"Indeed, a good bargain," answered Herr Bauer. "Yet, since I gave my permission for the villagers to build a small chapel on the hill outside Nesterhoffen, by laboring on their own time when they have finished their day's work for me, I find they spare themselves most selfishly on building my castle during the day so that they are most industrious at night. Or have you two wise and observant gentlemen taken no notice of this strange event?" questioned the vexed prince.

The two men from Nesterhoffen exchanged dumbfounded glances, for neither had observed what the prince was telling them.

"But an even larger problem caused by your chapel building has come to my attention," stated Prince Ludwig. "You must have noticed the bands of crusaders that have passed through Nesterhoffen this

Baron Otto

summer!”

Both Herr Bauer and Oskar Claus were quick to nod their heads in assent.

“Well, these heavily armed crusaders that you have so obligingly noticed at your inn, Herr Bauer,” said the prince, reminding Herr Bauer of how well his business was doing by his dealings with the crusaders, “have brought it to my attention that your chapel is not officially sanctioned by the High Bishop of Vienna. This, in the eyes of many of the more zealous of them, is a sacrilegious blasphemy!” The irate prince had risen from his chair and pointed an accusing finger at the two worried and frightened villagers. “And some of them have gone so far as to threaten the burning of the chapel and even the village itself to help cleanse my soul of this blasphemy!” The prince was almost shouting now.

By now, the two men were terrified and averted their eyes, unable to look upon their prince.

The prince had succeeded in his plan to humble these men but he did not wish them to believe him a ruler of harshness and no honor. After a few moments of silence to let the impact of his words strike home, he lowered the tone of his voice, saying calmly, “Yet, I am a reasonable man. Do not take undue offense. The fault lies partially with myself as well.”

With these words, the village elder and Herr Claus were somewhat reassured of the prince’s good intentions.

“But, for the sake of all of us, the building of your chapel must stop – at least until the High Bishop of Vienna arrives in Nesterhoffen to sanction it,” stated Prince Ludwig. “As you know, he agreed on my wedding day to come and give his blessing to the Castle of Nesterhoffen upon its completion. I see no reason why he might not be persuaded to sanction your chapel at the same time. Would this not be a satisfactory arrangement for all of us at Nesterhoffen?" asked the prince.

"Yes indeed, Your Highness!" quickly exclaimed a much relieved Herr Bauer, while Oskar Claus nodded his agreement fervently.

"Good! Now then," Prince Ludwig went on, clasping his hands in celebration of the arrangement, "as for these weeks of wasted work upon my castle, how do you propose to repay me, Herr Bauer?"

Herr Bauer could only stutter and stammer, for the question had caught him unprepared and without an answer.

Prince Ludwig was quick to silence the sputtering village elder as he answered his own question. "Perhaps those village workers who have been so slack at their work on my castle and yet so industrious while working on your chapel each night, might wish to find recompense in my graces by working two months of extra labor at night upon my castle. After all, I am due some payment for their wasted weeks of laziness. I should think that two months of industrious labor at night should be considered an adequate payment from the village. How say you, Herr Bauer?"

Herr Bauer gasped with relief and stammered, "Yes. Yes, Your Highness. Your decision is most kind, and I assure you the villagers of Nesterhoffen will work most diligently for you, both day and night."

"Excellent, Herr Bauer!" The prince was pleased. "I shall hold you to your word and make you personally responsible for the villagers' industry." The prince now turned to Oskar Claus.

"Now, as for you, Herr Claus. Since it was you who started all these problems for everyone, I think a special debt is owed me." The prince stared hard at the trembling carpenter.

Oskar Claus had never imagined that his seemingly simple request would cause these kinds of problems.

"For you, the added work at night labor shall be one full year," stated Prince Ludwig, sternly. "And what say you to that?"

The poor, shaken village carpenter could only agree; he had no one to blame for his problems but himself. "Yes, Your Highness. Whatsoever you wish." Oskar Claus said in all humility.

"Good! Very good indeed, Herr Claus! And here is how your nights of extra labor are to be spent," said the prince. "It has come to my attention that you are no small craftsman in the art of carpentry and that you do remarkably well at constructing small wooden toys for children as well. Is this true?" asked the prince.

"I think what rumors you may have heard about my skills are vastly overrated," answered the humble and modest carpenter.

Puzzled by the man's modesty, the prince posed a question to Herr Bauer, "What say you of this man's abilities, Herr Bauer?"

Herr Bauer was quick to respond and most emphatic. "Your Highness," he said, "all who know Herr Claus have nothing but the highest praise for his skills at carpentry! As for his ability to carve wooden toys for children, his work is so unique and beautiful that one has only to look upon the joyous face of any child who receives them."

This was all the answer the prince needed. Turning once again to the humble village carpenter, he passed his judgment. "Then I propose that your nights of extra labor for one full year, Herr Claus, be spent in making toys for the young prince or princess-to-be. Though," confided the prince, "I most heartily hope for a boy child."

"And now, what say you, Herr Claus?" asked the prince gaily.

"I should be most delighted to make the toys, Your Highness," beamed the happy and bewildered carpenter, as his spirits rose from the depths of fear to the heights of joyous relief. Nothing gave Oskar Claus greater pleasure and satisfaction in life than making small wooden toys for children. To see a small child's face brighten with joy and happiness when receiving one of his toys was worth more to him than all the gold in the castles of Europe.

The prince, too, was satisfied with these bargains. Now, he need not fear the wrath of over-zealous crusaders, and the extra two months of labor by the villagers at night would more than makeup for the lost work. And the toys that Oskar Claus made would bring hours of happiness and joy to both the toymaker and the prince's hoped-for son.

And so, the village of Nesterhoffen became once again a happy and harmonious place, especially in the first week of July of the following year when a boy child was born to the prince and princess and jubilation rang supreme.

Baron Otto

And the little chapel on the hill

sat alone and unfulfilled.

Just a skeleton of a dream,

a shadow of one man's will.

Chapter IV: From Light to Darkness

The boy child was named Johan Erik Gotthardt Von Nickolaus by the prince and princess, but he was lovingly called little Erik by the people of Nesterhoffen. He was a robust and healthy child, with his mother's hair, his father's eyes, and a set of lungs that could bellow loud enough to make a large elephant jealous.

Little Erik's appetite was immense, yet it was no match for his curiosity. Most of all, he delighted in the toys of Oskar Claus. The colored rattles and clink-clanks, the tiny pushcarts and pull clacker-ducks, small wooden soldiers and horses made him grin with delight.

Erik grew swiftly in size and beauty and his temperament was such that all adored him. On his first birthday, the child was surrounded by gifts beyond number: small gifts from the humblest and poorest peasants of Nesterhoffen to gifts of wealth and prestige from Kings Karl and Ewald. Yet, no gift delighted the happy boy more than the small wooden rocking horse made by Oskar Claus.

When Prince Ludwig or Princess Inga held and rocked the small child upon his rocking horse, his little face brightened with radiant joy. Many hours of each day were happily spent in this manner as little Erik never seemed to tire of his rocking horse.

The days turned to weeks and the weeks to months, and each brought more contentment to those who lived in Nesterhoffen, and none could imagine that this situation would ever change. But, as life itself is nothing but a series of changes, so it was for those who lived in Nesterhoffen. The changes that were about to take place in the tiny village of Nesterhoffen would change the world forever.

***

For sixteen-year-old Hana, working as a maid in the castle at Nesterhoffen was pure delight. The castle seemed to ring with laughter and joy, especially on this particular Christmas Eve.

Everyone about the castle and village scurried about with an exuberance of goodwill and smiling expectancy of Christmas Day's feasting ahead. Hana's own mind was blissfully preoccupied with these thoughts as she hastily cleaned and dusted the baby prince's room.

In Hana's haste and preoccupation she became careless. In stepping back from making the young child's bed, she stumbled on a toy soldier lying on the floor and fell heavily on the young prince's favorite toy, the small rocking horse, and broke one of its legs.

Dismayed at her clumsiness, Hana tried to repair the damage. Though she could get the broken leg to fit back together so that it looked unbroken, the strain of any weight upon the rocking horse would certainly cause it to collapse. Hana decided she must take the broken toy back to Oskar Claus on her way home from the castle that night and see if he could fix it for her.

This decided, Hana placed the broken toy rocking horse outside little Erik's bedroom door at the top of a steep, stone staircase. She planned to pick it up after she finished her remaining chores and take it with her when she departed. Unfortunately, for everyone in Nesterhoffen, poor Hana, in her excitement over the forthcoming gaiety of Christmas, forgot about the broken toy rocking horse and left it at the top of the stone staircase.

****

Long after Hana had finished her work for the day at the castle,

Princess Inga climbed the staircase with the sleepy young Erik cuddled snuggly in her arms.

As Princess Inga entered the young boy's room, she noticed the seemingly unbroken toy rocking horse standing outside her son's bedroom door. A smile came to her face as she thought of how much her young son loved the toy and how Prince Ludwig spent seemingly endless hours rocking the happy, laughing child.

Placing the young child in his bed, Princess Inga decided to return the toy rocking horse to the boy's room. She could think of no reason why it had been abandoned in the hallway. Before she left her drowsy son's bed, she noticed a chilly draft in the room. Since it was a cold, windy, and snowy evening, she decided to first get her child an extra blanket.

Going through the open connecting doorway to her and Prince Ludwig's room for an extra blanket was only a moment's space in time. Only the briefest few minutes would pass before Princess Inga returned with the blanket.

Little Erik drowsily watched his mother leave the room. Then, through the open door leading into the hall, he spied his favorite toy, the rocking horse. A smile lit his tiny face as he slid silently from bed and tottered out to his favorite toy. With a supreme effort of will and boyish strength, he climbed upon its back, and there he tried to rock himself for one last ride before going to bed.

Just then, Princess Inga returned to the boy's room with the extra blanket. Seeing the young boy's bed empty, her heart turned to ice, and terror filled her soul. Her panic-stricken eyes flashed about the room. Finally, she found her beloved young son astride the rocking horse in the hallway. Before she could call his name or take a single step, the broken leg gave way on the rocking horse, and the toy fell over, pitching the screaming child down the steep stone staircase.

Princess Inga's scream could be heard throughout the castle. The Christmas joy that had surrounded everyone in Nesterhoffen was to shatter and break upon a wall of grief and despair.

97

Just as tomorrow must follow today

and night shall follow the sun,

We go from light to darkness,

each and every one.

Chapter V: The Losing of a Child The Stolen Egg

Frantic, Princess Inga ran to her son near the bottom of the steep stone staircase; there, she was surrounded by those in the castle.

Those first at her side were Prince Ludwig, Horst, and Arno, each with a drawn sword and fiery eyes that searched for an evil culprit. But no culprit of dark desires was to be found… only the weeping form of Princess Inga as she bent to comfort her badly injured child. No sword would be needed to help him. Only a physician of great skill was required.

Prince Ludwig was the first to note the seriousness of the child's injuries. He himself had scars to prove how dangerous the accidents of youth can be. But his youth had held one advantage: an elder physician of great merit lived in his father's castle. At Nesterhoffen, there was no elder physician of great merit nor even a young physician of questionable merit. In fact, Nesterhoffen had no physician at all.

Prince Ludwig made the only decision he could. He had to save the life of his beloved son. "Quickly," he called to Horst and Arno. "Prepare a light sleigh and gather twenty of your stoutest men. We'll take the child through the pass and on to King Ewald's castle in Salzburg." Though he would have preferred to reach his father's castle in Wasserburg, he knew that, with the winter storm about him, his closest and only chance lay in reaching the Castle of Salzburg and the physician there. In any case, it would be no simple feat.

The pass to Salzburg was a deadly and treacherous route in winter, as for men trying to pull a sleigh through deep snow, even a small sleigh would be almost impossible. Yet, if they failed to try, the child's death was certain. Knowing this, their wills turned to steel.

With twenty of the strongest soldiers, Prince Ludwig, Horst, Arno and Princess Inga, who refused to leave the side of her child, departed in the cold, dark, windy snow to try and save the life of little Erik.

Ten men pulled the sleigh and followed the lead of Horst, while Prince Ludwig ran beside his wife, who cradled the warmly bundled child in her arms upon the sleigh. Arno and his ten men ran behind, until their turn came to replace the exhausted men in front.

On into the night and storm, they traveled. First, Horst and his men pulled and ran until their strength dwindled; then, Arno and his men pulled and ran until, once again, they had to switch places. Hour after tedious hour, the men pulled the sleigh.

When their strength was all but gone, and their bodies sought only to collapse and lie in the cold, clean snow, they struggled on. Their hearts were as the lion and they would not quit. They found a reserve of new energy, some deep well of unimaginable and unfathomable courage and strength to surge onward, ever onward.

Finally, they came to the treacherous mountain pass itself: a precipitous, slanting defile on the one side that ended far down at the frozen river and a sheer wall of towering snow-heaped mountains on the other side. It was a narrow defile of deep drifts of snow and threatening avalanches, a place of swirling snow-filled darkness and danger, a fearsome distance of two miles to relative safety at the other end of the pass.

The courageous party paused a few moments while Prince Ludwig checked with Princess Inga to ensure that all was well with her and the still-unconscious child. Arno and Horst took these moments to encourage the spirits of their tired men and warn them of the danger of loud noises within the pass. Any sound might start an avalanche that would be deadly to all. So, with great caution and difficulty through the deep snow drifts, they proceeded and slowly, with tremendous effort and care, made their way into this valley of death.

For almost the full two miles, they quietly struggled with the sleigh and their exhausted bodies, pulling and pushing onward in silent superhuman effort.

As their cause was almost won, their worst fears were realized. Tiny Erik became conscious. With a mighty bellow of youthful rage and pain, he brought the mountain down.

The avalanche that followed scattered them as leaves upon the wind. The sleigh was spilled and tumbled by its force, as were the men themselves.

Four men and the sleigh containing the child were lost to the walls of the rushing snow.

Hour after futile, frenzied hour, Horst, Arno, Prince Ludwig, Princess Inga, and the remaining sixteen men searched through the vast snowdrifts to no avail.

Through the torch-lit darkness of night and far into the gloomy gray, snow-filled day, they searched until each collapsed in turn from total exhaustion. Only Prince Ludwig refused to collapse. He continued searching in a frenzy of grief and disbelief until finally, Princess Inga went to him and, with tear-filled eyes, begged him to stop.

She had come to realize the futility of their puny human efforts against the vastness of the damage wrought by the avalanche and the impossibility of finding the small boy or the four men under the tons of snow that stretched in all directions about them.

With an enormous grief, the party turned and made its weary way back to Nesterhoffen. There would be no feasting on this Christmas Day.

Baron Otto

To lose a simple wager is pain enough for most,

but tis only from your pocketbook you pay for

futile boast,

But when your only child is torn from you apart,

there's nothing in this world you wouldn't give

instead,

For the loss is from your heart.

Chapter VI: Tale of the Unknown Woodsman

On that winter's snowy, windblown night a woodsman with his coverings of furs pulled tight about him tended his traps far in the forest. In time, he headed homeward over a frozen river through the narrow valley pass toward the great forest on the far side. There, he lived in a humble log cabin, secluded and alone. He was a hermit trapper who only came to Salzburg to trade his winter collection of furs each year in the spring.

Barely had he started through the defile when he heard the ominous rumble of an avalanche ahead of him. Quickly, he turned and ran back up the frozen river toward safety, and only by the narrowest of margins escaped the charging waves of snow.

After resting for many moments to calm his racing heart and make sure the avalanche had ended, he once more turned and trudged warily down the now snow-filled corridor toward his home. Not long did he walk before his acutely- honed sense of hearing caught the nuance of something strange upon the wind. His ears were trained to know all the whistles and whispers of the wind, and what he heard now was not of the wind's making but rather a distant sound of a wounded bird or small animal. With great caution and skill, he tracked the shifting sound through the swirling winter's night.

First, one way and then another, the sound came to him as the wind tried to deceive him. But the woodsman was not easily fooled. Soon, he found the source of the sounds. To his great surprise, when he raised his axe to put an end to what seemed a wounded fox's suffering, a tiny human leg and then a tiny human hand appeared. The befuddled woodsman stood there in shock as the wind played its best trick of all. It blew the fox's fur open and exposed the child beneath.

The helpless, broken child greeted this cold new outrage and the dumbfounded woodsman with a wail of rage.

As quickly as the woodsman's mind had stopped, it started again and his head was filled with impossible questions: Who is this child? How does he come to be lying alone in such a remote place?

"HELLO!" he hollered as he noted the boy's twisted broken leg. He quickly bundled him up in the fur hide of the fox skin. Where are his people? He wondered, his mother and father.

"HELLO? Is anyone there?" he yelled as he cradled the child to his bosom. Receiving no answer and afraid his loud voice would cause another avalanche, he did the only thing he could do; he slowly and carefully began making his way toward his cottage.

And thus, the woodsman carrying his burden through the valley and the party from Nesterhoffen far above, passed each other in the night without ever knowing of the others' presence.

Upon reaching his small log cabin, the woodsman quickly built a roaring fire in his fireplace. There, by its light and warmth, he tended to the wounded child. No small knowledge of medicine did he have, for in his way, he was a good physician and knew much about treating wounds with nature's herbs, barks, roots and mosses. Goodly stocks of these were always kept on hand for his own emergencies.

With many years of first-hand knowledge, he worked on the child. The boy was gravely hurt, with one leg broken and a forearm as well. Though the woodsman set the bones and placed splints on the limbs, he feared the worst from shock and pneumonia.

For two weeks, he barely left the child's side as he fed him hearty broths of grouse and rabbit laced with healing herbs. He soothed him gently with soft, encouraging words by the warm fireplace. Finally, the raging fever broke and the boy slept peacefully as his tiny young body turned to mending itself. By his side, the weary hermit woodsman smiled and slept at last. The worst was over; the boy would live!

Baron Otto

Let us hope that in the follies of

our own passing, we may find the

kindness of a good Samaritan,

such as the unknown woodsman.

Chapter VII: Banishment

When the exhausted, grief-stricken party reached Nesterhoffen, the word of the tragedy spread like wildfire; the entire village was shocked and numb with disbelief.

Slowly, the prince led Inga up the steep stone staircase toward their room to comfort her. At the top of the steps, his downcast eyes fell upon the broken rocking horse. He was quick to kneel and examine it while Princess Inga sobbed out the details of what had happened.

The prince's grief turned to anger and rage. Now, he saw the villain of his son's death as the careless toymaker who had made the faulty toy rocking horse with one leg so weak it collapsed under his small child's weight and sent him crashing to his doom.

So certain was Prince Ludwig about the evidence before him that he did not bother to check further. Instead, he stormed from the castle in a blind fury, heading for the house of Oskar Claus. Horst and Arno saw him leaving in this evil mood and hurried to follow him.

With a thunderous crash, the Clauses' door was flung open, and the raging prince charged in, bellowing insults and curses at the Clauses. Horst and Arno arrived at just that moment and grabbed the prince to hold him back. Ludwig was determined to kill the toymaker with his bare hands.

Crimson with rage, the prince wouldn't listen to calmer reason. He heaped blame after blame upon Oskar Claus – from the building of the chapel with its attending problems – to the shoddy workmanship of the toy rocking horse.

"I shall return within the hour," raged the prince, "and I will burn your house to the ground, and if you are still in it, so much the better!" he shouted. Then he tore himself loose from Horst and Arno and raced back to the castle to find a torch, while Horst, Arno, Oskar and Emma Claus stood in shocked silence and stared at each other in disbelief.

Arno was the first to come to this senses. Shaking Oskar's arm, he said, "Quickly, Herr Claus. You must leave here. Take what possessions you can and leave Nesterhoffen before the prince returns. His rage is beyond control. No one can stop him now!"

As if in answer to this statement, the prince could be heard shouting obscenities and blasphemies at God from afar.

The four of them quickly put what few things they could into the small sleigh that Oskar used for hauling firewood in winter. With these few meager belongings and Oskar and Emma bundled up against the winter's storm, the four of them raced to cross the toll bridge at the edge of Nesterhoffen. Here, Horst and Arno bade the Clauses farewell and good luck.

As Oskar and Emma Claus pulled the simple sleight with their meager, hastily-grabbed belongings away from Nesterhoffen, they turned for one last look at their village. What they saw were two smoking, flame-shot pyres where their cottage and the little chapel had stood.

A heavy silence and great darkness of despair settled over the Castle at Nesterhoffen and the once happy villagers who lived there. The lovely Princess Inga, in her solitude and grief, refused to leave Little Erik's room, not wishing to see or talk to anyone. Each night, her sobs could be heard as she cried herself to sleep.

Prince Ludwig, whose kindness and generosity to the villagers of Nesterhoffen had made him so loved, became a tyrant of barely suppressed rage. In his grief and anger, he struck out at those very people who shared his grief and loved him most.

As each day passed, the prince devised a heavier and crueler method to exact his revenge upon the poor innocent villagers of Nesterhoffen. He doubled and then tripled their taxes. One-third of all future harvest of hops would belong to the castle. One out of three newborn animals would belong to him. Increasing tolls were charged for the use of the bridge at Nesterhoffen, be the user traveling merchant or local villager. And on and on, the list of punishments grew with each passing day.

Worst of all, the prince banished God from Nesterhoffen. The prince had lost all his faith. There would be no more Christmases; neither would the burned-out little chapel at the edge of the village be rebuilt.

The once-happy village of Nesterhoffen became a mire of grief and self-pity. The faces of the villagers became blank and forlorn. Not one smile was seen there, not one laughing child. Only silence and misery reigned.

The curse from the ancient gypsy hag was coming to pass. The egg that was the joy and prosperity of Nesterhoffen had been stolen.

Baron Otto

That the end justifies the means?

That the means justify the end?

Best you think more clearly,

for reason always bends.

Chapter VIII: A Journey into the Wilderness

Through the long, cold night, through the next day, and into the following night, Emma and Oskar Claus pulled their sleigh, hoping their exertions would keep them from freezing to death in the eerie snow-covered forest, which seemed to go on forever.

The second night, they were both near collapse when they heard the far-off baying of wolves. As they listened, the frightening sounds grew nearer, ever nearer.

Oskar went to the sleigh, took the only weapon he had – his axe for chopping wood – and stood protectively in front of his wife. But Emma was not so frightened that she would allow her husband to fight alone. She went to the sleigh and returned seconds later to stand beside her husband with a formidable straight-edged garden hoe.

There, on a narrow mountain path, surrounded by huge impenetrable forests, they waited with all the courage they had for almost certain death. Then, a strange thing happened. The clouds that had shrouded the evening in snow and darkness, slowly parted. The spot on which they stood and all about them was washed in the light of the brilliant moon. Into this arena of light, not twenty paces ahead of them, staggered a small, exhausted doe. There, she collapsed, totally spent in her efforts to outrun the wolves.

Barely had the doe fallen when a magnificent buck emerged from the woods and gently prodded the doe with his enormous rack of horns, willing the doe to stand and run. But his efforts were in vain for the doe was so exhausted she did not have the energy to rise.

With sides heaving from his long and terrifying chase, the buck placed her close behind him and, refusing to run off into the woods to safety alone, prepared to battle to his death.

The woods about them rang to the fearful howling of the wolves as a half-dozen of the ugly, snarling brutes erupted from the forest. One launched an immediate attack on the proud but exhausted stag. The wolf was quickly driven back by the deadly antlers. Another wolf dashed in to hamstring the stag from behind, only to fall in a pool of its own blood as its head was split open by the stag's flashing hooves. Yet another wolf attached, only to limp back, gored in the neck and side.

Magnificent as the mighty stag's defense was, the outcome remained inevitable. This mighty monarch of the woods must eventually tire, slow, and be overcome.

Emma Claus realized that once the wolves had finished with the deer, she and Oskar would be next. Grasping her husband's arm and pulling him forward, she told him, "Come, we must fight the wolves."

With a surprise that caught the wolves unaware, Oskar and Emma Claus joined the terrible struggle of life and death in the brightly lit arena. As if he had gone berserk, Oskar scythed his way through the wolves with this axe, while Emma gashed and gouged with her garden hoe until, finally, they stood close by the fallen doe, facing the last of the ferocious wolves.

Now, the doe's protectors numbered three who stood in a small circle about her. And the wolves went wild in frustration and rage. Time and time again, they attached. Yet each time, they were beaten back, and each time, there were fewer wolves left unwounded or alive. Until four of their number lay dead upon the snow, and the other two could barely slink away to lick their wounds in total defeat.

The magnificent buck snorted his disdain at the retreating wolves, and then he dropped his head in exhaustion as he stood on trembling legs.

Emma slowly sank to her knees, also in utter exhaustion.

In time, Oskar pulled himself together and went to the sleigh to look for some food. He found a loaf, of course, dark bread, which he brought back to the circle. Soon, Oskar, Emma, and the buck and doe were eating and renewing their strength as they sat on the lonely, narrow path amid the great snow-clad wilderness.

And, as if by the glow of some gigantic immortal eye, they were bathed in the circle of light from above.

Baron Otto

For all who must face a journey into the wilderness,

be sure that you take along one thing above all others

and are prepared to share it.

– <u>Courage.</u>

Chapter IX: The Smallest Samaritan

As the foursome lingered over the bread while they regained their strength, the stag became restless, circling the group with this head thrown high; he sniffed the wind and snorted defiantly at the dead wolves. Oskar Claus was quick to judge his meaning. "Emma, we must leave here. Soon, more wolves may smell the blood. We must get far away from here," he said urgently.

Emma Claus was not one to argue with logic. She hoped never to have to fight a pack of ferocious wolves with only a garden hoe in her hands, not ever again!

Soon, the Clauses were both in harness, pulling their sleigh with all the speed they could muster. Out of the circle of light and back into the snowy darkness of the path, they went with the buck and doe tagging along. They were thankful for the falling snow; it would cover their tracks and whatever scent the wolves might hope to follow.

Now, the doe walked beside them, and the stalwart buck ranged a few yards ahead as if to guide them. Always alert, the buck constantly sniffed and occasionally rushed ahead to stop and look and listen until, once again, the group behind him drew near.

Hour after hour, they traveled, and it seemed the sleigh hardly weighed enough to notice. Several times Oskar had to look back just to convince himself it was still there.

Only once did they stop to tuck Emma into a snug blanket on the sleigh, for she was near exhaustion and could barely stand. The deer stopped also and waited for Oskar, until once again he was ready to move ahead.

Sometime during the night, they left the path that would have led them to Salzburg. But, as the snow and darkness kept Oskar's vision dimmed to all but a few feet about him, so, too, did the weariness and exhaustion dim his mind. Trustingly, he plodded along, following the stag ever deeper into the vast forest, until at last, his body stopped, and still leaning into the harness, he slept.

At dawn's first gray light Oskar Claus was awakened by the friendly doe that seemed to find great pleasure in licking the stubble of Oskar's sprouting new beard. Slowly, Oskar's fatigued and weary senses came into focus. Then, with a sudden rush of fear, he became fully awake. All about him were trees and hills. He stood, not on a path made by men and carts but on a simple, narrow deer trail deep in an unknown forest.

With the snow still falling lightly about him, he tried desperately to see the path to Salzburg. But none was to be found. Only deer trails that led in all directions were visible. Hastily, he ran behind the sleigh, where Emma slept in blissful ignorance of their plight. The snow had covered their tracks; it was almost as if some giant hand had plucked them up and placed them far away in the middle of nowhere. The hopelessness of their situation overwhelmed him, and Oskar sank to his knees in the snow, his head in his hands, and moaned unashamedly in despair.

They were alone and lost, deep in some unknown forest with no way of finding their way out and barely enough food for one small meal.

Oskar sobbed in quiet despair, that he had brought his beloved wife to such an end. They would die slowly of starvation in this great forest or freeze to death if they were not killed by wolves. "Oh, what a giant fool I was," moaned Oskar. "To have followed these wild deer all night without so much a question in my mind of whether or not it was a wise thing to do!" He thought. "And now, what have I gotten us? I might as well have murdered poor Emma with my axe, for surely I have killed her with my foolishness!"

Then, Emma was there, kneeling beside him in the snow, holding him to her and whispering gently, "Oskar, my love, do not fret so. Everything will be all right."

But Oskar, in his anguish, blurted out that everything would not be all right. They were hopelessly lost, without food or shelter, and unable to retrace their way back to the path to Salzburg. "We will surely starve, freeze to death or worse," he lamented.

Emma had a strong faith in her husband whom she loved even more than her own life. She was bothered not by the fickle twists and turns of life's meanderings. These things always seemed darkest before they brightened.

She realized that Oskar's fears and hopelessness were related to his fear for her safety and not his own; if he were alone in this situation, he would go on until the last spark of life and be drained from him with never a thought of giving up or turning back.

"I think liebchen that you have worked enough for one day," Emma soothed lovingly. "What with fighting wolves and pulling a heavy sleigh all night? No wonder you're weary in mind and soul." Then, Emma led him back to the sleigh.

"You must get some rest now. I'll build a fire and make some soup. Then, we will decide what is to be done, my husband."

"But the wolves," protested Oskar…

"Don't worry about the wolves," she said, pointing to the two deer that stood close by watching them. "We have two of the best watchdogs in all of Europe."

Soon, Oskar fell into a deep but fitful sleep. Emma covered him with a blanket and kissed his forehead, whispering, "Sleep well, my love."

Though she knew well the desperation of their predicament, Emma still found it within herself to hum softly as she busied herself building a fire and putting on a pot for soup. All the while, she found moments to stop and talk to the deer that were browsing on what tender bits of tree branches they could find nearby. Whenever she stopped what she was doing to talk to them, they cocked their ears to listen.

Emma let her husband sleep even after the soup was done, for she didn't have the heart to wake him. She used the time to melt enough snow to quench the deer's thirst. Toward noon, as near as she could tell in the light of the falling snow, she woke her husband. The buck had been growing restless, and not knowing its meaning, she thought it best to tell her husband.

Oskar awoke with a jump, eyes flying open and one hand grabbing for his axe before he realized that his arm was being shaken by Emma and not the wolf in his fitful dreams.

Emma was so startled she fairly jumped back with surprise.

"I…I thought you were a wolf, "said the sheepish Oskar.

"Well," chided Emma, "I may not be as pretty as I once was, Herr Claus, but I certainly do not think I look like some old wolf!"

"No, Emma," he smiled, "to me, you grow more beautiful every day." And getting up from the sleigh, he gave Emma a warm embrace. Then, with a sly smile, he added, "And certainly much better looking than any old wolf, though there was one last night that wasn't altogether unappealing." He quickly ducked his head to avoid the large snowball Emma threw at him.

All of this commotion drew the two curious deer closer to camp, and before Oskar could settle down to eat his soup, the young doe came over and nudged his arm. By now, Oskar and Emma knew the doe had grown quite fond of having her ears rubbed.

The buck snorted his disdain at this nonsense and went back to browsing on the nearest tree.

Over his soup, Oskar became serious once again and asked, "Emma, what should we do now, do you think?"

Emma had no way of knowing what to do. Though she realized how desperate they were, she also realized she was woefully inadequate as a woodsman and that whatever chance of survival they had would rest solely upon her husband. Since that was the case, she didn't want to burden him with worrying so much about her that he couldn't face the problem squarely and with resolve.

"Oskar Claus," she admonished, "for twenty-seven years of marriage, you have told me what to do." – "Wash my good pants for Sunday, Emma!" – "Roast a duck for our guests on Wednesday, Emma!" – "Don't forget to weed the garden, Emma!" – "Now you face a little problem, and all of a sudden, you say, "Emma, what should we do?"

Shaking her finger at him, she continued in a stern voice, "I'll tell you this much, Herr Claus, if God wants us to die in this wilderness, then we shall die, no matter what we do. But," she softly added, "I think that if he had wanted that to be, then we would not have survived the wolves last night.

I think he has other plans for us, so I'll trust in what you decide."

After saying her piece, Emma sat upon the sleigh with crossed arms and a determined expression on her face.

After studying Emma's stern countenance for a short while and thinking about what she had said, Oskar's face slowly broke into a smile and then a wide grin.

"And what do you find so funny, Herr Claus?" asked Emma.

"Not funny, my love," replied Oskar. "It's just that sometimes you make the happiness bubble up inside me." And so saying, Oskar stepped over to Emma, took her into his arms and kissed her with deep love and devotion.

The big buck snorted at all this human foolishness and paced nervously about.

Within a few moments, the two humans, with their friends, the deer, were once again on the march. With all of Oskar's ability as a woodsman, he tried to keep them headed in an easterly direction where he hoped they would reach Salzburg.

The deer, though, grew more and more loathe to stay near them in the directions and paths that Oskar took. Finally, as evening descended and the snow fell harder, the two deer were gone and returned no more.

Realizing the futility of trying to find their way through a vast, unknown forest on a dark, snowy evening, Oskar and Emma did their best to make a camp for the night.

Many hours later, as the two lay huddled asleep on their sleigh beneath their animal skin blankets, Oskar awoke to a strange and distant sound.

Rising to hear better, he awoke Emma, who whispered in a frightened voice, "What is it, Oskar?"

All about them was darkness with hardly a wind and only the faint sound of falling snowflakes.

"Shhh," whispered Oskar. "Listen."

As they both strained to hear, the faint jingling of bells came to them. The sounds drew closer. These were not church bells calling from a far-off steeple. Nor were they cowbells, though that seemed closer to the truth. Oskar and Emma had never before heard such delicate-sounding bells.

"Jingle, jingle, jingle," the bells went, as ever louder and closer they came. Then, off in the trees nearby, they saw a feeble and flickering light passing swiftly through the woods. Before either of them could become frightened by whatever danger this might be, they shouted, "Hello, hello, over here! Please help us! Over here!"

The flickering light stopped and then came quickly toward them. Much to Oskar and Emma's great surprise, the first thing to appear was their friend, the mighty stag.

About the stag's neck was a leather collar. And from the collar were two long reins with tiny jingling bells attached. At the other end of the reins, with a torch in one hand and a peaked and pointed red hat on his head, stood a tiny little whiskered man upon two stubby slats of wood. Oskar and Emma Claus were stunned and speechless.

Not so the tiny man. "O-Ho," he grunted gruffly. "So you're what's had Blitzen all worked up in a frenzy. I'll bet it is! I'll bet it is!"

"Ho-Ho, pilgrims who've lost their way," he gleefully laughed as he unfastened the wooden slats from his feet. "I'll bet you are! I'll bet you are!"

And deftly did he move, this strange tiny fellow as he happily chattered away.

"Ho, Blitzen, good fellow. Be off now. Away! Away!" He unfastened the stag's harness and pushed him away. Off like a shot, the mighty stag bounded, soon lost in the night and the forest. There, the three stood by the light of the torch that the tiny man had stuck in the snow, each more curious than the other.

"Ho– I mean, who are you?" Oskar Claus sputtered, still not sure he wasn't dreaming.

"O-Ho!" cheered the tiny fellow, as he danced from one small leg to the other. "The pilgrim has a voice. So clever! So clever!"

Then he stopped his antics to stare at the Clauses, saying sternly, "I'm a dwarf, and this is my forest, and you'd best behave yourselves, or I'll cast a spell upon you!"

Emma had stood silent till then, but she could no longer restrain herself. To think that their friends, the deer, had gone to find help for them and returned with this tiny, funny man was most bizarre! And that this humorous-looking fellow, in his absurd little pointed hat, could possibly find a spell that would be more dangerous than their present situation; well, it was just laughable! So Emma laughed and laughed and laughed.

Now, Oskar Claus caught the humor of the situation, and he began to laugh.

At first, the tiny dwarf was vexed at the laughing couple. He jumped furiously from one foot to the other. This only caused the Clauses to laugh harder until the perplexed dwarf began to laugh. And they all laughed so hard they held their sides with pain, and still they laughed.

So, on that fateful snowy night, the three became the best of friends: Oskar Claus, his wife Emma, and a funny little dwarf named Jon Kaan. And the clouds parted, and the snowstorm and darkness finally came to an end.

Baron Otto

It is not the size of the man,

but the size of his heart that

counts the most.

Chapter X: A Haven in the Woods

That night, the three waited out the dark by a warm and cheery fire. Each told their stories of how and why they had come to meet in this strange and unusual manner. By dawn's first feeble light the tiny dwarf named Jon Kaan led the Clauses to his home.

Stopping on a hilltop and nodding to the little valley below, Jon Kaan pointed to his home. Then, jumping joyfully about, he said, "Ho-Ho, that's my beautiful home. That's my home!"

Oskar and Emma Claus looked at each other in consternation, for the six tiny shed-like buildings they saw seemed hardly fit for animals, let alone people. And the nearby village they had hoped for was nowhere to be seen.

Slowly, they made their way down the snow-clad hillside. As they closed upon the group of ramshackle huts, their joy at being saved fell to impossible lows. Surely, no human being could live in such miserable houses.

As if to disprove their thoughts, the huts suddenly burst with life. Out poured at least two dozen tiny little men, women and children. Soon, Oskar and Emma were surrounded by a happy, joyous, cheering group of dwarfs, all rejoicing in the return of Jon Kaan, and none but the little children seemed very curious, at first, about Oskar and Emma.

Jon Kaan, their elder, told his story to them as he hopped from one foot to the other in their midst. The tiny throng "Ouuued" and "Ahhhed" at the heroic tale he spun. When he told how Oskar and Emma Claus had saved their deer, Blitzen and Dancer, from the wolves, with nothing but a woodman's axe and a garden hose, the throng grew silent with awe. With a collective cheer of amazement, the little group of dwarfs rushed to the Clauses, each trying to out-thank the others with their boisterous gratitude.

Bewildered, Oskar and Emma Claus were smothered in a rush of affection, and their hearts were melted by the warmth and kindness of the tiny people. All thoughts of witches and devil's pawns disappeared; they were among friends.

Soon the Clauses were squeezed inside the tiny hut of Jon Kaan, where his short, wide little wife, Elfriede, introduced them to the Kaan children. From oldest to youngest, they were Able, Gable, Marla and, finally, the little wide-eyed and excited two-year-old, Karla.

While Elfriede made Emma comfortable, Jon Kaan took Oskar aside and asked him if he would go to a meeting of the village men with him. There it would be decided what best could be done about Oskar and Emma's plight. Oskar readily accepted.

The two gathered the other tiny men of the village and walked a considerable distance through the snow until they reached an enclave in a hill. Winding their way between the towering sides about them, at last, they came to its end. They entered a circle with sheer rock walls on every side and one enormous pine tree in the center of the circle.

This was where the tiny dwarfs came to find guidance in all their most important decisions. This was their tabernacle. No word of dishonesty was allowed in this place.

First, Jon Kaan asked Oskar to retell his story of the night before, so all those present might be able to judge his plight. This Oskar did from the beginning until his presence there.

The dwarfs responded, each in turn.

"We could lead the Clauses back to the path to Nesterhoffen," said one.

"But what good would that do?" said another. "Surely they can't return there."

"They could go the other way to Salzburg," suggested yet another.

"But they have no money, no friends, no relatives in Salzburg," refuted the second dwarf.

"Well, they can't stay here," said the first dwarf. "We have barely enough food and shelter for ourselves. Why, look at their size," he continued, pointing to Oskar's rather rotund belly. "They'd eat three times what you or I might eat, and where could they possibly sleep?"

"But they would have no food or shelter in Salzburg either," replied the second. "And, when word has reached King Ewald of the death of his daughter's child, their lives would be forfeited."

The dwarfs continued to argue in an effort to find a solution, until Jon Kaan, who had been silent, stood up. "They can neither go backward to Nesterhoffen nor onwards to Salzburg," he stated. "Either direction would bring them only suffering and loss. The winter is upon us, and all roads to travel beyond those two places are impossible to reach.

No, this man and his wife have done me a great service in saving the lives of Blitzen and Dancer. Without Blitzen, I would be unable to plow my field next summer, and many of us would starve from the loss."

The dwarfs took heed of what he said, and Oskar Claus, the most: he had never heard of deer being tamed and used to pull a plow.

"This man says he's a carpenter," went on Jon. "And I dare say we need one badly. I say that for his help in carpentry work, we each share in providing his food. As for a place to sleep, they shall sleep in my home." This said, the tiny, funny-looking man with his absurd little peaked red hat sat down.

Nary was heard a dissenting word among them. All of them saw the wisdom of Jon Kaan. All that remained was for Oskar to agree. With his heart overflowing with gratitude at the sacrifices these little men were making for him and his wife, Oskar readily accepted.

They stayed in that place and conversed a while longer, deciding how the needs of the tiny village could best be served by Oskar's skill at carpentry. It was decided by all, that the shed which housed the pigeons and rabbits, their one lowly milk cow, and which gave protection to their pet deer, should be their first concern. On these animals, they depended for their very survival, and so feeble was this shelter that many animals would surely die if the shed was not repaired.

With these decisions made, they made their way back to their houses. All were greatly pleased and excited, with one possible exception, the first dwarf who was called "Roary" by the others. Though his real name was Reggie Reemiss, he was always first to roar his disapproval at all things; and had been nicknamed "Roary." As Roary sulked along, he was sure the others would all regret their decisions.

When the men arrived at their huts, they were welcomed by their wives and children, who had decided to celebrate the day's events with a simple but hearty feast. Since Emma Claus had a great deal to do with the cooking, it was considered, by all, the best meal any of them could ever remember. Even the obstinate Roary was pleased; he ate everything in sight and said not a single word of objection.

On the following day, Oskar Claus and the four village men, with their eldest children went to work repairing the rickety shed that housed the animals. Within a week, the shed was extended and repaired. Now, it was roomy and snug, enclosed from the weather.

Next, they started work on the huts. Oskar's plan was to build a large cabin attached to Jon Kaan's house on the one side and the barn they had finished on the other side. From there, they would build out, and each of the remaining four huts would be attached to this main building as well. Thus, the entire compound would be attached to one large building. It would serve as a community center for meals and meetings, while the attached huts would be converted to family bedrooms. Also, it would provide a bedroom of sufficient size for Oskar and Emma, who were only able to sleep on the cold and drafty floor of Jon Kaan's hut.

Everyone was greatly pleased with this idea and could hardly wait to get started. All, that is, but Roary Reemiss; he insisted that the whole plan was impossible and would surely tumble down upon their heads in the first strong wind.

Despite his objections, the work began, and so industriously did the dwarfs' work that by the first of April, the main building was finished. What they lacked in size, the tiny people more than made up for in their boundless energy and enthusiasm.

To celebrate the completion of this building, a feast was planned for the first Sunday of that month. All the women helped in preparing it with Emma elected as head cook. Though it was not the sumptuous banquet one might imagine, it was a considerable treat to these extremely poor but noble dwarfs. Roasted rabbits and pigeons, they had. Potato dumplings and barley soup, they had. Hot fresh bread and lots of thick, rich gravy to sop it in, they had. And their humble but happy banquet was a great success. Everyone enjoyed themselves, and laughter filled their souls with love and joy—all that is, except Roary Reemiss. Though he stuffed himself most outrageously, his disparaging grunts could be heard behind every grumbly mouthful.

And there came on earth a humble carpenter of Nazareth,

and to all of mankind, he brought a special gift.

A thousand years later, another humble carpenter appeared

in the small, little village of Nesterhoffen.

And from his haven far in the woods,

he, too, brought a special gift to all of mankind.

Chapter XI: A New Friend and an Old Friend

By the end of April, the work on the buildings where the dwarfs lived was drawing to an end. Oskar Claus was growing more concerned with each passing day. He doubted his wife would agree to remain there and live in the simple fashion of the dwarfs. He reasoned that surely she would wish to be away that summer to a more normal life in a regular village. Before he consulted Emma, he wanted to study this problem himself so that he might come up with some logic and reason to guide them in whatever her wishes might be. Oskar's love for Emma was so great he would go anywhere or do anything she desired.

Thus, on the last day of April, Oskar went off by himself to think. He decided to go to the Tabernacle of the Dwarfs and meditate alone. Winding his way back through the chasm, Oskar arrived at the base of the mighty pine tree. In this secluded spot, the air was still cold, and the spring warmth had not yet entered. The mighty pine tree was still draped in icicles and puffs of snow.

Oskar dusted the snow from a nearby rock and seated himself in contemplation. As he dropped deep in thought, the wind sent gentle puffs through the pine tree, and the icicles chimed softly. "Don't go!" they seemed to say. "Please don't leave," they chimed. "We need you, Oskar Claus," the tree whispered softly.

Oskar found no answers there, only more confusion and a deep abiding knowledge that he loved these simple, poverty-worn dwarfs. They had come to be the family and children he never had.

With head lowered in deep thought, Oskar rose, and, clasping his hands behind him, started to pace about the majestic pine tree.

Halfway around the pine tree, his reverie came to a startling halt. There, lying in the snow, hidden beneath the tree's branches, were two large pink eyes staring at him. Oskar was not only surprised but concerned at what possible creature this could be.

Very carefully, for he did not want to arouse the creature's anger, he checked for telltale tracks the creature might have left in the snow. But only a few old rabbit tracks could be seen. Certainly, no animal could have gotten beneath the tree without leaving fresh tracks in the snow, he reasoned.

Possibly a bird that's fallen from his nest, high above, he thought next. Yet, he could think of no bird that had two large, soft pink eyes.

Gathering all his courage, Oskar reached a hand carefully into the branches to spread them so he might plainly see the creature. Then, with a flurry of motion, the creature lunged, grabbed Oskar's thumb in its mouth and began to suckle!

To Oskar's shock and surprise, he found a tiny little albino fawn attached to his thumb. Gathering the poor, abandoned and starving infant deer into his lap, he nursed it with his thumb. With his free hand, he gently stroked it and spoke soothingly to it while he studied this tiny apparition. Certainly, it wouldn't be more than a few days old, he guessed. Yet, none of the old and fading tracks in the snow could possibly have belonged to the mother. Judging by the way it feverishly sucked his thumb, the poor fawn had not been fed in quite some time.

As he glanced about in consternation, Oskar happened to look up at the top of the pine tree. As he did, he discovered where the fawn had come from. Near the top of the tree, where it stood closest to the cliffs above, a path had been swept through its branches from top to bottom. Obviously, the tiny fawn with his pink eyes, white coat, and shiny red nose had somehow fallen from the cliff to the pine tree and swiftly through its branches to lie unhurt, though abandoned, below.

"Well, little fellow," he cooed to the fawn, "it seems I've come to the right place for heavenly guidance. Surely, there is nothing that needs heavenly guidance more than you, and you are also here." Oskar said as he stroked its soft ears.

"I think my simple problems can wait, while we take care of yours." So saying, he took the fawn gently in his arms and carried it back toward the home of the dwarfs.

The dwarfs, busy with the tasks Oskar had assigned them before he left for his walk in the woods, were not overly concerned with Oskar's delay in returning. Only Jon Kaan grew nervous as time slipped by. Jon had noticed how his friend had grown more contemplative of late. It bothered him that Oskar did not share his problems and troubles with him and the others. So it was with great delight and relief, when he saw the smiling form of Oskar coming back through the woods that he cheered.

"O-Ho! Here comes my friend, Here comes Oskar Claus!" he shouted gleefully while trying his best to jump from one foot to the other atop the slanting roof he was working on.

All the dwarfs turned happily to greet Oskar's return. But it was Roary who first spied the tiny fawn in his arms. "He's killed a deer," cried Roary in rage. "I told you he was no good. I told you so!"

The dwarfs grew silent and still; among them, the deer were sacred friends, and none of the dwarfs could imagine hurting one.

But Oskar only smiled as he drew near the dwarfs. Then, he looked straight into the accusing eyes of Roary, saying, "Shh. If you don't quiet your foolish howling, it's you that may scare this poor fawn to death." Then he placed the tiny white fawn on its feet so that all might see that it was alive.

Great was the surprise and excitement of the dwarfs' camp that day. An albino fawn was a rarity that few had ever seen. All wished to pet and hold him. But the fawn only had a liking for his newly-adopted friend, Oskar Claus, and was skittish with the rest.

Oskar took the fawn into his and Emma's room. Emma made a feeder from an old glove and bottle, and with fresh, warm milk from the cow, Oskar fed the fawn. The children came to peek through the open doorway and giggled with pleasure at the sight. That night in their bed, with the fawn sleeping contently on a small layer of straw nearby, Oskar and Emma Claus had a long and serious discussion.

They both learned that neither of them really wanted to leave these happy and loving dwarfs. They decided to ask the dwarfs' permission to live with them permanently. This decided, they found contentment and slept in each other's arms.

The next morning, when all had gathered in the meeting room for breakfast, Oskar and Emma stood up. Oskar placed an arm around Emma's shoulders and asked the gathering, "We'd like to know if we could stay on and live here with you or if you would rather we left and made our home elsewhere?"

The dwarfs were shocked and stunned that Oskar and Emma had even considered moving away. But not Roary; as usual, he was the first to speak out.

"Hurrrumppp." He chortled. "Work's too much for you, no doubt. Can't keep up, quitters the both of you!"

Before Roary could get his second breath and go on, Jon Kaan said, "Ho, for myself, I say stay," and raising his arm and hopping about, he asked the rest, "How say you? How say you?"

All the dwarfs stood, men, women and children, and raised an arm and hollered, "Stay. Please stay!"

Little Karla, tears in her frightened eyes, toddled over to them, grabbed Oskar's hand and pleaded, "Please, Oskar Claus, don't leave us."

Only Roary, who had not voted, still sat. When all were silent and then turned to him, expectantly, he rose. Slowly lifting his arm, he exclaimed, "They're such a lousy carpenter and cook no one else would probably have them!"

So, the vote was unanimous, and the day was marked by great happiness and goodwill. Each found joy in the decision, but none more so than Emma and Oskar Claus.

***

By the first of June, with the building completed, the dwarfs turned their attention to gathering their various trade goods. Fox and rabbit furs from their winter traps and medicinal roots from the forest made up most of their wares.

Each day, one of the dwarfs made the day-long trek to a lookout that provided a view of the road between Salzburg and Nesterhoffen. It was here, each year, they waited for the arrival of the one man who did not scorn them and think them pawns of the devil, an old merchant peddler they knew as Rudolf.

Soon, it was Oskar Claus's turn to go with Jon Kaan to keep watch at the lookout. As they arrived that morning, they saw on the path below the merchant's cart and donkey.

"O-Ho, that's his cart! That's his donkey!" said Jon Kaan, jumping about with glee. But no merchant was in sight.

Quickly descending from the lookout, the two men approached the standing donkey cart. As they came closer, they saw two legs sticking out from beneath the cart and heard an assortment of colorful curses.

"Damnable hunk of junk on wheels," they heard, "Most worthless collection of misused firewood I've ever set my eyes on," scorned the hidden voice.

Oskar sensed he knew that voice; even the cart and donkey looked familiar to him. Standing by the two legs that disappeared beneath the cart, Oskar turned to Jon Kaan and asked, "You say this man's name is Rudolf. Do you know his family name?"

"Ho, for sure, for sure," replied the dwarf. "His other name is Ishman. Rudolf Ishman is he."

Upon hearing his name, Rudolf was quick to wiggle from beneath the cart. "Jon Kaan!" he exclaimed upon seeing the happy dwarf. "Why do you go about sneaking up on poor old peddlers and scaring the wits out of them? And who is this stranger you've brought?" Ishman didn't recognize his old friend, Oskar Claus, beneath the full white beard he had grown since their first meeting.

"O-Ho," squealed the happy dwarf as he jumped about. "This is my friend, Oskar Claus, the best carpenter in all the world. And his wife's the finest cook. Yes, they are, oh, yes, they are!"

Then it dawned on the old peddler Ishman; this was his friend who had helped him fix his broken cart and had given him a beautifully carved wooden toy a year before in Nesterhoffen. "May Heaven be blessed! It is you, Oskar Claus, "he said as he hugged and slapped Oskar's back. "I was just on my way to Nesterhoffen, where I was hoping to find you. I have a proposition to put to you that could make us both wealthy men...."

"Ho-Ho," interrupted Jon Kaan, "the old peddler's been in the sun too long. I bet he has, I bet he has!"

"But how does it happen you are here with this jackal of the woods?" asked Ishman, paying no heed to the dwarf.

Oskar explained how he and Emma had come to grief in Nesterhoffen and ended up living with Jon Kaan and the dwarfs.

"So tragic," sympathized the old peddler. "Then perhaps my news will cheer you some." With that, Ishman narrated his tale.

It seemed that Ishman had gone on to Vienna after leaving the Claus' home in Nesterhoffen the year before. There in the great city, he had come upon hard times. He had been forced to sell the handsome toy soldier Oskar had given him in order to buy food. The merchant who bought the toy soldier for a goodly price was so enthralled by the fineness of its craftsmanship, that he had made a bargain with Ishman to purchase all the toys like it that Ishman could get.

"And so, you see," exclaimed Ishman, "Why I was on my way to see you in Nesterhoffen! If you were to turn your talents to making these toys, I could haul them to Vienna and sell them for you. And the prices the merchant is willing to pay, even splitting the profits between us, we could grow rich!"

"A noble idea, my friend, "said Oskar as he nodded. "If my life had not changed so drastically last winter, I should have welcomed this venture. But unfortunately, all my tools were lost when Prince Ludwig burned our cottage. I have nothing to work with and no money to purchase new tools."

"Alas," moaned Ishman. "And I have no money to help, either."

"Ho-Ho," gleefully chattered Jon Kaan. "What about me….? What about me?"

"Don't pull our leg, Jon Kaan," admonished Ishman. "You have no money either!"

"And certainly no tools I could use," added Oskar; he knew well what crude implements the dwarfs owned.

"Ho! Certainly no money and no tools either!" he chuckled. "But what of our winter's trade goods? My fine pair of friends – what of them? Would they not purchase the tools you need? I bet they would, I bet they would!" The tiny man jumped gleefully about like a toy on a spring.

"But, of course!" cried Ishman, his old legs jumping for joy. "I could use your winter's trade goods to buy what you'd need in Salzburg. Why, I could be there and back within the week!"

With a handshake all around, the bargain was sealed and each would share equally from the profits.

Baron Otto

While Oskar stayed with Ishman to help fix his broken cart once again, Jon Kaan raced back to the dwarfs' house to fetch their winter's trade goods.

Ishman was as good as his word, returning with the needed tools before the week was done.

The dwarfs and Oskar Claus used their large meeting room for a workshop to make the toys. Since it took old Ishman a month to make the trip to Vienna and back, he had time for only three trips that year before the snow and cold made his journey no longer possible.

Because their workmanship was so fine, all their toys were bought at once in Vienna. By summer's end, the dwarfs owned a healthy new cow, six pigs, four sheep, the gift of Ishman's half-lame old donkey, and three large bolts of bright red cloth. In gratitude to Ishman, Oskar named his albino fawn Rudolf.

For there is nothing more

comforting than an old friend.

And no better way to find one

than by making a new friend.

Chapter XII: The Beginning of a Legend

The unknown woodsman also went to Salzburg that spring to trade his winter's furs. Though the boy was not really strong enough to go along, the woodsman had no choice but to carry him on his back. At the outskirts of Salzburg, he hired an old woman, living alone in a cottage, to watch the child while he traded his furs at the market square.

There, he came to hear the story of how the Prince and Princess of Nesterhoffen had lost their small child in an avalanche. He immediately knew whose child he had found.

Yet, the hermit trapper kept his silence; he knew not what to do. The boy had come to mean so much to him and had been his only companion through all the days of that year. He was like a son to him, and the poor hermit's heart was torn apart by indecision.

What should I do? What should I do? Cried his mind as he raced back to the cottage where he had left the child. When he saw the young boy's smile greet him, his heart melted. He could not bring himself to return the child to its rightful parents.

Gathering the boy and the goods he's traded for, he made his way hurriedly back to his simple log cabin. There, he spent many months in anguish and torment. What should I do…? What should I do? He agonized.

***

In the haven in the woods, the dwarfs had been quick to learn the skills of toy-making from Oskar Claus. Soon, they were making a considerable supply of these highly-prized toys. Their imagination was such that they were always conceiving new toys and designs. Soon, it became quite clear to them that by working all winter, they would have a most impressive stockpile for Ishman to sell the following year.

It was Emma who asked them if perhaps they might have a few toys to spare. In Ishman's travels that summer, he had brought word of how disparaging and unhappy life had become in Nesterhoffen. Emma could only think how sad the children must be there.

It was decided that on Christmas Eve of that year, Oskar and Jon Kaan would go to Nesterhoffen in the safety of the night and leave toys for all the children there. To this end, they built a sleigh that could be easily pulled through the snow by their friends, the deer. Knowing, as they did, each child of Nesterhoffen they made a special toy for each. All was in readiness by early December.

***

In Nesterhoffen, the long year of suffering and grief was undiminished. As Christmas once again drew near, the villagers secretly decided to hold a midnight prayer on Christmas Eve at the little burned-out chapel on the hill to ask for God's forgiveness and blessing. They had nowhere else to turn, and their burdens were almost unbearable.

Prince Ludwig had heard a rumor of the secret midnight service and made his secret plans as well. I'll teach those worthless peasants a painful lesson! He told himself.

***

So it came to pass that one year to the day of Little Erik's tragic accident, he was once again on the snow-covered path that led from

Nesterhoffen. The unknown woodsman, unaware of what day it was, had finally decided that the boy should be with his rightful parents. Without further delay he had bundled up the boy snugly against the snow and cold and set off for Nesterhoffen with the child on his back.

Late that night, while the snowflakes were gently falling, the woodsman reached a point only a mile or two from Nesterhoffen when he was overtaken by a strange apparition. Gliding quickly through the snow was a sleigh pulled by deer. Sitting upon huge, lumpy sacks in the sleigh was a funny little dwarf, while riding on the sleigh's back runners was a chubby, white-bearded man all dressed in red. The unknown woodsman was overtaken so quickly that he had no time to react to this strange vision.

"Ho-Ho!" cried the dwarf as he pulled on the reins and stopped the sleigh beside the bewildered and frightened woodsman. "I'll bet you're going to Nesterhoffen. I'll bet you are! I'll bet you are!"

The woodsman, for all his strength and courage, stood still and trembled with fear.

The jolly-looking fat man with his red suit and white beard was quick to calm the woodman's fright. He explained that they were on their way to Nesterhoffen on a mission of charity. Then, Oskar bade the woodsman to ride on the sleigh.

The woodsman complied, for he knew not what else to do in his confusion. By midnight of Christmas Eve, the sleigh arrived at the outskirts of Nesterhoffen.

There, Oskar asked a favor of the woodsman: to keep his sleigh and deer safe while he and his friend, the dwarf, carried their bags of toys into Nesterhoffen. Again, the woodsman complied.

While those two were gone, the woodsman took the bundled child from his back, and the two of them soon became friends with the deer. The woodman's fears lessened somewhat as he watched the joy on the face of the child as they both would pet the deer.

***

Oskar Claus and Jon Kaan entered what seemed, at first, to be the deserted village of Nesterhoffen. When they happened to notice what looked like the entire village of men, women and children all gathered on the far distant hilltop where the burned-out remains of the chapel stood. Apparently, the entire village had gone there to hold a Christmas Eve, midnight service in honor of the birth of the Christ Child.

In the quiet of the village, Oskar and Jon Kaan went about their work. They had decided that the best place to leave the toys was beneath the pine tree that stood next to Otto Bauer's Inn. Otto had always refused to chop this tree down because of the protection it provided his inn from the cold north wind during winter times. This full-green pine stood draped in snow and icicles and had plenty of room beneath its branches for Oskar's purpose. While Oskar placed the toys, Jon Kaan threw brightly colored streamers upon the tree so that the returning villagers would notice it and find the toys.

It was not long before they had finished and returned to their sleigh.

The woodsman, seeing them coming, quickly covered the child and returned him to the position on his back. He still had many concerns about dwarfs and witchcraft, no matter how friendly these two appeared. He wanted no harm to befall the child that he had grown to love.

"If there is someone special, you seek this night in Nesterhoffen?" Oskar inquired of the woodsman. "I suggest you try to find them at the gathering taking place at the burned-out chapel on the hill." After giving the woodsman directions, Oskar wished him a Merry Christmas and a pleasant goodnight. Then Oskar and Jon Kaan departed with their deer and sleigh.

Pausing in a clearing on a nearby hill, they stopped to look back at the village of Nesterhoffen. It was on this very place where the four ancient hags had cast their curse upon Nesterhoffen a few years before.

The woodsman entered the village and saw at the far end, the Castle of Nesterhoffen. From the castle came what appeared to be the entire garrison of troops, all dressed out for battle. Off they charged toward the spot where Oskar Claus had told him to find the gathering of villagers at the burned-out chapel on the hill. As he neared the castle, a woman appeared and rushed from its gate; so hastily did she come that she ran right into the woodsman.

Quickly grabbing her arm to stop her, the woodsman asked, "Begging your pardon, My Lady, but where might I find the Prince and Princess of Nesterhoffen?"

The woman was quick to reply, "I'm the Princess of Nesterhoffen. But I have no time to talk. The Prince has taken the garrison, and I fear what evil he has planned." With this, she tore loose from the woodman's grasp and was about to run away.

"But I have your child!" cried the woodsman.

Princess Inga froze in her tracks. "What foul jest is this?" She cried, turning back to the woodsman.

"No jest, dear lady," soothed the woodsman as he took the bundled child from his back. "I was traveling far below the avalanche that night a year ago, and the child was swept almost into my arms. See for yourself; I speak the truth."

As the woodsman uncovered the child, Princess Inga stepped forward to look. The recognition of her child was such a shock that she fainted on the spot.

Bundling the child on his back once more and gathering the princess in his arms, the woodsman made his way to the burned-out chapel on the hill.

The woodsman arrived just as the garrison had surrounded the villagers and gathered them in a tiny circle in the midst of the burned-out chapel. Prince Ludwig had gone among them and was about to pass his sentence and punish them, when through the milling, fearful throng came the woodsman, Princess Inga, being carried in his arms.

Seeing his beloved wife limp in the woodman's arms, the prince forgot all else and rushed to her.

"Fear not, Your Highness," said the woodman to the prince. "She has only swooned at learning your child still lives." Then, he placed the slowly reviving princess into the trembling arms of the startled prince. Once again, he removed the boy child from his back and uncovered him.

"It's him," sobbed the prince. "It's Little Erik!" – It's him – He's alive. May God be praised! It's Little Erik. He's alive and well!"

***

The happy, rejoicing people of Nesterhoffen made their way back to the village. But there they were met by another surprise. A brilliant light shone down through the clouds and fell in a circle about the pine tree by Herr Bauer's Inn. The ribbons seemed to glisten magically, while the snow and icicles radiated a brilliance as if they had a life of their own. And beneath the tree, they found the many toys.

The tears were feely mingled with the blessings on that long ago, snowy Christmas night.

And like the glow of some immortal giant eye, the light came down from above and bathed the rejoicing people of Nesterhoffen in its splendor. Yet the strangest thing of all...was that on that night, there was no moon at all!!!!!!!

The curse placed upon Nesterhoffen was broken forever.

For some, the end;

For others, a new beginning!

Show me those children with no parents, no

home, no hope, no love.

No food to sustain them, no warm clothes to cover them.

Show me those orphans whose pillows are made from tears,

whose dreams are empty darkness.

Show me those children that no one cares

to share their love with, that I might be their brother.

For I will share my bread to ease their hunger,

the warmth of my coat will give them comfort

from the cold and storm.

They shall have my love and no longer cry from loneliness.

And the joy of life to come will ring ever in their dreams.

This story is dedicated to the orphans of the world, along with what help I might be able to give them… that they may someday know the joys of Christmas.

BARON OTTO